Push Back

Push Back

Karen Spafford-Fitz

James Lorimer & Company Ltd., Publishers
Toronto

James Lorimer & Company Ltd., Publishers acknowledges funding support from the Ontario Arts Council (OAC), an agency of the Government of Ontario. We acknowledge the support of the Canada Council for the Arts, which last year invested $153 million to bring the arts to Canadians throughout the country. This project has been made possible in part by the Government of Canada and with the support of the Ontario Media Development Corporation.

Cover design: Gwen North
Cover image: Shutterstock

Library and Archives Canada Cataloguing in Publication

Spafford-Fitz, Karen, 1963-, author
  Push back / Karen Spafford-Fitz.

Issued in print and electronic formats.
ISBN 978-1-4594-1375-7 (softcover).--ISBN 978-1-4594-1376-4 (EPUB)

    I. Title.

PS8637.P33P87 2018   jC813'.6   C2018-902569-7
                                              C2018-902570-0

Published by: Distributed in Canada by: Distributed in the US by:
James Lorimer &   Formac Lorimer Books   Lerner Publisher Services
Company Ltd., Publishers   5502 Atlantic Street   1251 Washington Ave. N.
117 Peter Street, Suite 304 Halifax, NS, Canada   Minneapolis, MN, USA
Toronto, ON, Canada   B3H 1G4   55401
M5V 0M3   www.lernerbooks.com
www.lorimer.ca

Printed and bound in Canada.
Manufactured by Friesens Corporation in Altona, Manitoba,
Canada in July 2018.
Job # 245780

For my dear, ridiculous brothers —
Jack Jr., Derrick and Paul

Chapter 1

Under the Bridge

Keep moving, Zaine. Just keep moving.

I'm muttering the words over and over. It's one of the first things I learned on the streets. Keep moving, and don't get caught off guard — especially after dark.

The last three weeks have been a crash course in survival. I've learned a lot of things the hard way. You can't assume empty cars are abandoned, because their owners might come back in the middle of the night. Offers to sleep on someone's couch can come with strings attached, like being expected to have sex with the couch's owner. And shelters aren't places where you should try to catch any sleep. The only time I stayed at one, someone stole my extra hoodie, two pairs of socks, and my last twelve bucks.

My legs are heavy as I shuffle down the grimy sidewalk. The wind blows a plastic bag against my legs. I'm too tired to kick it away. I veer toward the stone building to try to get out of the wind. A groan nearly makes me jump out of my soggy running shoes.

In the darkness, I almost trip on the edge of a sleeping bag. The guy huddled inside it is barely visible beneath the doorway. "Sorry, man," I say.

I flip up the collar of my jacket. *God, will this Edmonton winter never end?* But I can't think too far ahead. I just need to keep stumbling forward.

I'm at the edge of the city when my backpack slips off my shoulder. Hoisting it back up takes more strength than I have. My eyes are heavy and I'm afraid I'll drop onto the street right out here in the open. So when the street leads onto a footbridge that stretches over the river, I circle around to the path underneath it. In the dim light, I can barely see the concrete wall running across the bottom of the bridge. The narrow space between the dividing wall and the bridge is mostly hidden. It also looks like it's protected from the wind.

I lean forward and start climbing up the rocky slope toward it. I curl my fingers around the metal wire laid over the rocks. When I get to the dividing wall, I peer over the side. The space behind it is big enough for me to fit inside. It's filled with soft earth and gravel. There are no clothes or food wrappers. No sign at all that someone lives here. I nearly sob with relief. Maybe this is my lucky break. I could use one of those for a change.

I pull myself in and roll onto my side. I can almost stretch my legs right out. I tuck my backpack under my head. I want to stay awake for even a few minutes — just to be extra cautious. But even as that thought bumps through my head, I am drifting off to sleep.

✱ ✱ ✱

"What the —?"

That's all I hear before it starts. A fist collides with the side of my head, then my throat, then back to my head. One punch, then another. I call out as I try to cover my face.

"This is my turf!" a man growls. "Mine!"

In this tight space, I can't move. I can't defend myself from the guy who's cursing me out. Not from the punches, not from his sour, boozy breath in my face. The whole time, he's punching me again and again. Each blow sends a shockwave of pain firing through me.

"It belongs to me!" he yells.

I can barely see the outline of his body. He's climbed up higher. When he raises his foot to stomp down, I grab it and hold on. Then I give it a twist and I push it away from me. He roars as he tumbles down the rocky slope. His body lands with a heavy *thud* on the path below.

I roll out from behind the concrete wall just as the guy gets to his feet and starts back up the slope. I lunge toward him to try to knock him over. But my shoe catches in the wire mesh and I pitch forward, landing right at his feet. He grunts and puts the boots to me — one hard kick after another. My body recoils in a hot, hard spasm each time.

I'm trying to crawl away from him. I open my mouth and spit something out. Blood. Then I gag as the next kick catches me in the gut. Then the back of the head.

Of all the fights I used to get in at school, I never lost a single one. I always just let the rage take over. And I have a *lot* of rage to draw on. But out here, the rules are different. Because actually there are no rules.

"Sorry." I force the word out through my bloodied mouth.

He gives me another kick.

"It's yours." I spit the words out.

"Damn right it is," the man snarls. "So get out of here!"

I pull myself off the ground, my hands clutching my stomach. I'm weaving along the path. It's only when my face scratches against something cold and damp that I realize I've fallen down. I don't want to move. I *can't* move. So I just lie there — feeling all those kicks and punches merging into one massive hurt that's taking over my entire body. Through it all, a voice is running through my head.

Zaine, you stay here with Aunt Sarah. I'll be back in a month.

"Mom? *Mom?*" I realize that the thin, crackling voice is mine.

"Mom," I say, "I can't wait any longer."

Chapter 2

Voices

Even without opening my eyes, I know something is different.

I shift slightly, then I gasp from the pain that shoots through my body. What startles me even more is the softness underneath me. And the voices.

I think about opening my eyes, but I don't have the energy. The voices tugging at me will have to wait — except they aren't letting me ignore them any longer.

"Zaine. Zaine? You need to wake up now."

I slowly drag my eyes open. A brown face above me is smiling. A crease forms between her dark eyes as she looks down at me.

"My name is Dharma," she says. "You're safe here in the hospital. Someone has been waiting to talk to you."

A moment later, a new face appears.

"Mom?"

Even as the word slips from my mouth, I know I'm wrong. It's not Mom. But with her sandy brown hair and blue eyes, this woman looks a lot like my mom.

"Aunt Sarah."

"How are you doing, Zaine?" She doesn't wait for an answer, which is just as well. "The doctor said you were pretty beat up. You were in shock when they brought you here. Some cracked ribs, too. We'll know later about a concussion." She pauses. "At least your jaw isn't broken. Gosh, I've never seen such a black eye in my life."

"How did I . . ."

"Someone found you at the edge of the city," Aunt Sarah says. "The police said it was a homeless man. They know him from a downtown shelter where he often stays. He's the one who made the call."

A homeless man did that for me? He must be one of the kinder people out there. Most of the people I saw for the three weeks that I was sleeping rough were either mean, or they just ignored me. I guess they all have their own problems to deal with, just like I do. As for that guy who beat me up? I shudder. Then I grit my teeth as pain cuts through me again.

"The police found your learner's permit in your coat pocket," Aunt Sarah says. "They phoned me right away."

"How long . . ."

"You've been in the hospital for two days now." Aunt Sarah runs her hands through her hair. "I've been driving into Edmonton to see you since then. You're lucky that man found you in time."

Lucky? Me?

"The doctor will probably release you from the hospital in the next few days."

"But —" I have to dig up every word from a deep well in the back of my brain. It's a hard, slow process. Still, a picture of me going back out on the street fills my mind. I won't survive out there again. I just know it. But I can't find the words to explain.

"The police got in touch with your mom," Aunt Sarah says.

Mom? Now she really has my attention.

"Your mom called me back right away," she says. "Beth has decided to move back to Melton Grove at the end of the month. She's going to get an apartment for both of you."

An apartment with Mom?

When Mom dropped me off at Aunt Sarah's place, she said she'd be back to pick me up in a month — once she had "figured some stuff out." That was four years ago. We've hardly heard from her since then. And she's coming back? Maybe my luck is turning after all.

"When the doctor releases you," Aunt Sarah continues, "you can move back in with me. Until your mom arrives in town, that is."

Melton Grove is about thirty minutes from Edmonton. I should be relieved about moving back in with Aunt Sarah and my little cousins. Something doesn't make sense though. I lie extra still and let the scene play out in my head. The scene where I got kicked out of her house.

Now I remember. It was Rob, Aunt Sarah's husband, who had done it. In some ways, Rob was probably right when he said I have a lousy attitude. But right from the start, he made it clear that he didn't want me living with him and Aunt Sarah. Things got worse once the twins were born. Rob was always waiting for me to do something wrong so he had an excuse to come down extra hard on me. And the guy is no angel himself. He kept dropping by Melton Grove High School. He said it was to make sure I wasn't skipping classes. But I'm sure it was more about him wanting to check out the girls. I still remember his eyes latched onto their boobs and their butts.

Get your crap and get out of here!

That's what he yelled at me when he kicked me out. So I'd grabbed the little bit of cash I had on hand. I'd loaded up my backpack and caught a bus into Edmonton.

I look up at Aunt Sarah. She's still checking out my battered face.

"But — Rob," I say.

Aunt Sarah takes a tight breath. "Rob doesn't live with the twins and me anymore. I found some emails he had sent to other women on dating sites." She dashes away some tears. "Like, to younger women. About hooking up with them. It was sickening. So I sent him packing."

"He's gone?"

"He's gone," Aunt Sarah says.

Oh, thank god!

I never thought just talking would be

so hard. But my eyes are growing heavy. My forehead is itchy. When I reach up to scratch it, I realize it's covered with a bandage.

"I need to get home to the twins," Aunt Sarah says. "Mrs. Kriegson is looking after them."

Mrs. Kriegson, the grumpy next-door neighbour. *Jeez, the poor kids.*

I've missed Carter and Lawson. For the past three weeks, I tried not to think about them. It made everything harder to think that I wouldn't see them again. But then I'd spot a Dairy Queen and remember how crazy excited they got about an ice cream cone. I'd remember how cute they looked with more ice cream on their faces and down their shirts than in their mouths. Then everything would hurt even more.

"Get some rest," Aunt Sarah's voice cuts into my thoughts. "I'll come back again soon."

She leaves and I start thinking about how Mom is finally coming back to Melton Grove. We used to have lots of laughs together. Like when I'd pretend I accidentally drank her wine from the fridge instead of milk, and that I was too drunk to find my bedroom. Mom must have known that I was doing that just so I could get out of going to bed. Still, she laughed every time.

The best nights were when Mom would stop what she was doing and say, "That's it. I'm bored." Next thing I knew, we were going out to meet some of her friends — even on school nights.

I can still hear her big laugh and her words. *Let's go find a party, Zaine*, she'd say.

Those were good times for sure.

As I drift off to sleep again, I can feel a smile flitting across my face. I can't believe our little family of two will soon be back together again.

Chapter 3

Rage

Carter is driving his little ride-on tractor around the couch where I'm sprawled out. Lawson has scribbled another picture to show me.

"A cow!" Lawson shoves the paper at me. It looks just like the butterfly he showed me two minutes ago.

"Coolest cow ever," I say. "Right on, buddy."

His face lights up.

"Are you two letting Zaine rest?" Aunt Sarah calls from the kitchen.

"Yes."

"We are."

That seems like a lie. But maybe in their wacky little three-year-old world, that doesn't even qualify as 'bending the truth.'

This is pretty much how I spend my days now that I'm home from the hospital. Given all the punches and kicks I took, the doctor was surprised I didn't get a concussion. My ribs are healing well, and I've been up moving around more. That's probably why the twins keep forgetting that I can't always play with them or answer their millions of questions.

I've been watching the calendar closely. Just two days now until Mom moves back to Melton Grove. After four years, I don't want Mom coming back to a kid who can hardly bend over and tie his shoelaces. So I've been trying extra hard to get better. I'm starting to get a bit of exercise too. I even left the house a few days ago to pick up some boxes from the grocery store to pack my things in. I need to be stronger for when Mom gets here.

"Come on, you two." Aunt Sarah steps out of the kitchen. "Time to get ready for bed."

"No!" They say it together — the same little-kid whine in both their voices.

"No arguing," Aunt Sarah says.

Carter and Lawson look over at me.

"Sorry," I say. "I can't help you with this one."

They groan and follow Aunt Sarah to their bedroom. This is my cue to get some packing done. It's way easier when the twins aren't around to check out everything I'm trying to put into the boxes.

I've packed a lot of my clothes. Plus, I've taken down my posters and my photos from the walls. My bookshelf is mostly bare. I'm stacking all the dirty glasses and plates from my dresser when the phone rings. Aunt Sarah grabs it right away. Meanwhile, I kick my socks and T-shirts from the floor into a pile to throw in the washing machine later.

I'm taking the dishes into the dishwasher

when I pass by Aunt Sarah. She's still on the phone. With every word, her voice is growing angrier. "Beth, you'll have to tell him yourself."

Beth? That's Mom!

"Tell me what?" I ask.

"Just a minute," Aunt Sarah says. "Zaine is right here."

She takes the dishes and passes me the phone, then she steps into the kitchen.

"Mom?" I say. "Hey, what's up?"

"Zainey." She's practically purring over the phone. "It's so good to hear your voice, honey. You doing okay?"

"Yeah," I say. "Lots better. What did you want Aunt Sarah to tell me?"

Mom doesn't answer.

"It's almost March thirty-first," I say. "You know what that means . . ."

"Actually, we need to talk about that," Mom says.

A knot starts to tighten in my stomach. I drop down onto the couch. But my knee is bouncing and it won't stop.

"I've packed most of my things," I say.

Bounce, bounce, bounce.

"Zaine, honey," she pauses. "I'm afraid, uh —"

"That you'll be a few days late?" My throat has gone dry. I sound like a lost little kid. I swallow hard while I try to find my real voice again.

"Actually," Mom says, "I've met this special guy. He treats me real nice, Zaine. I'm going to be staying here after all."

"So, you're not coming back?" I'm clutching the phone in a white-knuckled death grip. "Do you want me to go there instead?"

Mom pauses before she speaks again. "For once," she says, "things are going great for me."

She completely avoided my question. I suddenly realize what's happening. She doesn't want me there with her either!

"Seriously, Mom?" I take a deep breath. "Did you really just say that things are going *great* for you?"

Mom gives a high-pitched laugh. "Yes,

Zaine," she says. "I did."

A wave of steam rushes into my head. I'm trying to keep my eyes fixed on the white wall across from me. I need to keep everything from turning red and explosive.

"How do you think things are going for me?" I ask. "Any idea, Mom?"

No answer. And she owes me that. Instead, Mom starts babbling on about how *special* her guy is. "And he has three kids — *three* of them, Zaine."

Just focus on the white wall.

"I *swore* I wasn't going to get involved again with a guy who has a houseful of kids."

Keep breathing.

"Because," she continues, "I hardly need a bunch of kids to raise."

"No, you sure don't," I say. "Especially since you're not even raising your own kid."

But I don't think Mom even hears me. She's still going on about her special new guy and her fabulous life. God, I was such an idiot to believe she wanted to live with me again.

"What's his name, Mom? You know — Mr. Wonderful?"

"His name is Jake." Mom gives that strained laugh again. "Mr. Wonderful — ha! Zaine, you're as cute and funny as ever."

"Cute and funny *as ever?*" I say. "How could you possibly know that? You haven't seen me in four years. You've hardly even *phoned* me!"

I leave some empty space hanging in the air between us. I'm hoping she'll realize how lousy this situation is for me and maybe change her mind. Still, she doesn't say anything.

When I finally speak up again, my voice is low and shaky. "Where are you?"

"Vancouver." Her cheery, upbeat voice makes me feel even sicker. "You should see the ocean and the amazing waterfront and the beaches here. You'd love it."

A lush, beautiful picture forms in my head — a picture that's exactly the opposite of boring, beige Melton Grove.

"Yeah, I bet I'd love it." My voice is rising.

"But I'll never know, right, Mom? Because I don't fit into your plans."

"Zaine, listen to me. It's just better if you stay with Aunt Sarah a bit longer because —"

I can't listen any more. I slam the phone down. I'm shaking and the white wall is tilting in front of my eyes.

Then I realize something. Even after what just happened on the phone, I still want Mom to come back. As pissed off as I am, if she were to phone back and say she's changed her mind, I'd still move in with her in a heartbeat. How pathetic is that?

Aunt Sarah steps into the living room. She's twisting a faded yellow tea towel between her hands. "I'm sorry, Zaine," she says. "Beth has always been . . ." she pauses. "She's always just been *Beth*."

I'm trying to process what she means by that, when I remember something Aunt Sarah said earlier. *You'll have to tell him yourself.*

"You already knew," I say. "And she wanted

you to tell me. She wanted you to do her dirty work for her."

I know that it isn't Aunt Sarah's fault. Still, a hot, dark rage is filling my head. I must have been louder than I realized because Lawson is standing in the doorway. He's rubbing his eyes and his lips are trembling. I need to leave before this turns any uglier. I slam the wall with both hands. Then I bolt toward the door.

The last thing I hear as I sprint down the driveway is Lawson crying and calling my name.

Chapter 4

The Shed

I run hard to try to keep ahead of the anger. My left knee still hurts from when the guy attacked me under the bridge. But I can't slow down.

When I left the house, I didn't think about where I was running to. I feel the heat streaming past my temples and I can still hear Mom's voice in my head. I can't go back to Aunt Sarah's yet.

Then an image pops into my mind. There's a shed where I used to go after Rob and I had some of our major blowouts. It's at the edge of the ravine, not far from here. I'm sure it's someone's art studio, and it's always calm and quiet there. That's where I'll go until the rage passes.

Gravel crunches under my feet as I run down the laneway behind the school. A few turns later and I'm at a little shopping plaza. The hair salon, the laundromat, and the corner store look more run-down than ever. A broken store window is partly covered with a sheet of plywood. Dark-blue and orange tags are spray-painted across it.

I veer behind the shops down into the woods. Heavy layers of leaves and mud are soon caked into the treads of my running shoes. Tree branches swat at my face. In the semi-darkness, the winding path has me feeling dizzy and turned around.

Just as I'm ready to explode, the path starts to weave upward. A rail fence is suddenly in front of me. I partly climb, partly step over it.

Then I run the last steps up out of the ravine. The garden shed appears up ahead.

As I jog toward it, I picture how orderly it is inside. The neat stacks of canvases, rows of paintbrushes in tin cans, and faded blue-jean colour of the walls have calmed me down every time. In some ways, I'd come to feel like this shed was partly mine. The rage inside me is already starting to fade.

I give the door a push. It usually swings open right away. But tonight, it's not budging — not even on the second try. Sweat trickles down the back of my neck. *What's the matter with this damn door?*

I slam my whole body against it. The door gives way and bangs open with a loud *screech*. I flip on the light switch.

My breath catches in a dry, hoarse gasp as I take in the room before me. Heaps of garbage bags are shoved against the back wall. A pile of boxes leans toward the centre of the room. White, plastic garden chairs are stacked in the corner with an old bicycle propped against them. Flowerpots and gardening tools are sticking out of a plastic milk crate. A toolbox is partly open and a cracked, leather punching bag has slid into the middle of the floor.

What the hell?

Everything about this is wrong — just like my whole life. Why does nothing ever stay the same or work out like it's supposed to? Not with my mom. Not at school. Not even here in this shed. Why does everything have to be so damn complicated?

That's the last thing I remember before a heavy curtain of rage slips over my eyes. Pressure is building inside me, choking me until I can hardly breathe.

Suddenly, I'm kicking the punching bag. Once, twice, then again and again. I shove the boxes over and slam the bike against the wall. The front tire clatters to the floor. I upend the boxes and crates. Books and sports equipment and screwdrivers are all a jumble by my feet.

I kick and stomp through masses of papers as though they're dead leaves from the ravine.

When I finally stand still, my T-shirt is drenched in sweat. I pace around the room until my breath starts to slow down. That's when I take in the complete mess around me. *Shit.* This is not what I came here to do tonight!

I push some boxes to the side of the room. I lean the bike back against the wall. I set the wheel beside it. Then I pick up a wrench. I'm looking for a place to set it down when I hear a branch snap outside.

Someone's coming!

I reach up and switch off the light. Beyond the window, a flashlight beam is bouncing up and down. Whoever is holding that light is almost at the door. And that's my only way out!

"Who's in here?" The voice is gruff.

So this old guy owns my shed now? And *this* is what he's done to it?

The flashlight beam lands squarely on my face as he bursts in the door — just as I'm twisting my body sideways to slide past him. He grabs onto me and the light veers crazily around the room. Parts of his face light up in the jagged beam. I see flashes of grey hair. A scar below his cheekbone. A tightly clenched jaw.

Shit, he's built like a cement truck!

Any time he can catch a breath, he's cursing me out. "You little shithead. Damn punk."

I'm struggling to get away from him. But he's shoving me backwards — slamming my body against the wall. I push back as hard as I can until we're in the doorway again.

Both of us are panting hard. We're nose-to-nose now and his breath hits me square in the face. Whatever he was just drinking takes me back to the night under the bridge. I can smell the street guy's stink and sweat and his nasty, boozy breath hammering me in the face, just like he hammered me with kicks and punches. I start to gag as nausea washes over me.

Then I realize I'm still clutching the wrench. I jab it into the guy's side. He grunts

and releases his hold. *This is my chance!* I push
past him and sprint toward the ravine. At least
it shouldn't be too hard to outrun this old guy.

"Why you little —"

His voice is right behind me! *What's with that?*

As I weave through the pine trees, I can
still hear his heavy breathing. It's even darker
down here now, so I barely see the rail fence.
Just in time, I throw my front leg over, then
I snap my other leg around. I realize I'm still
holding the wrench. It's slowing me down. I
need to get rid of it. I turn my body and fling it
Frisbee-style away from me.

A stream of swears and a heavy crash ring
out from behind me. The wrench must have hit
the old boozer. And unlike me, he didn't clear
the fence.

I keep running hard, my ankles catching
in ruts and slipping on the heavy mud. When
the plaza appears up ahead, I burst out of the
ravine. I wait until I'm past the school before
slowing to a walk.

I'm shivering in my sweaty T-shirt as I creep back into the house. Aunt Sarah is snoring softly on the couch. I peek into the twins' room. Lawson and Carter are both asleep too.

As I tiptoe into my bedroom, Mom's words start running through my head again. *I've met this special guy. It's just better if you stay with Aunt Sarah a bit longer.*

I drop down onto my bed. My whole body feels heavy. As for that old guy, I wonder if he made it back to his house okay.

Then again, to hell with him. He'll have to take care of himself, just like I've always had to.

Chapter 5

Melton Grove High

After the late-night struggle with the old guy, I'm exhausted. I guess I haven't fully recovered from the attack under the bridge. But I'm starting to feel better. And I've been helping Aunt Sarah, like with making dinner and cleaning up. And as always, there's no ducking the twins and their millions of 'why' questions every day.

Why my shadow sneeze too?

Why snow melt?

Why chocolate milk so yummy?

I try to answer Carter and Lawson as best I can. Meanwhile, I have my own questions. Like now that Mom isn't coming back, is Aunt Sarah still kicking me out at the end of the month? Because if so, that's tomorrow. It's hard not knowing one way or the other, but I'm too afraid to ask her.

"You know, Zaine, you need to get back to school."

I jump. I didn't hear Aunt Sarah come into the kitchen. She's looking at me through red-rimmed eyes. I heard her and Rob fighting on the phone last night. "Don't give me that crap!" she kept repeating. At least it looks like Rob won't be moving back in again. Thank god for that.

"You've been away from school for too long," Aunt Sarah says.

I open my mouth to tell her that I've missed too many classes. That I'm going to fail everything anyway. But this doesn't feel like the right time to argue.

"I don't know if they'll take me back," I say. "Like, at school, I mean."

I was passing most of my courses before I just disappeared from school. But I'd been in some fights too. I doubt the teachers or the principal will be overjoyed to see me again.

"Then that can be the first thing you ask the principal when you go there this afternoon."

Something in Aunt Sarah's voice tells me that saying 'no' isn't an option. I choke down a few pieces of toast.

Thirty minutes later, I'm staring at the red brick building. I wonder if there's anyone here at all who I haven't scared off by my famous rages. If I had any friends here, I'd be making bets with them about how long it'll take Mrs. Tang to say there's no room for me here. My guess is she'll send me away in less than ten minutes.

✻✻✻

The secretary at the main office tells me to wait out front until Mrs. Tang is free. I'm trying to ignore

all the surprised looks as students pass by. I'm sure
word is getting around fast that the psycho with the
crazy temper has turned up back at school again.

I'm trying to figure out how long it's been
since I was last at Melton Grove High. I left
school when Rob kicked me out. Then I was
on the streets for nearly three weeks. It's been
almost four weeks since the guy attacked me
under the bridge. It's taken me that long to
recover from it. That makes seven weeks. I shift
in my chair and I check out Mrs. Tang's posters
about Cambodia while I wait.

Mrs. Tang finally steps out of her office.
Much of her dark, choppy hair is spiked
straight up. At least that hasn't changed.

"Hi, Zaine," she says. "Good to see you
again."

I doubt that's true. But whatever.

She motions me into her office.

"Zaine, I'm going to get straight to the
point." She runs her fingers through her chunky,
beaded necklace. "As best I can tell, you are on

the brink of dropping out of school for good. It sounds like you're on a crash course to disaster. Back onto the street. Jail. You name it."

"How —"

"Your aunt phoned the office earlier this morning."

I should have known Aunt Sarah wouldn't trust me to make my way here. Then again, if she's going to toss me out, why would she bother calling the school at all?

"I realize," Mrs. Tang says, "that it's hard coming back to school. Especially after you've been away for a while. I admire your courage in returning here today. I hope it's a sign that you're committed to making some better choices."

Actually, it's just a sign that I'm trying to keep my ass off the street, Mrs. Tang.

"I have some ideas about how we might proceed," she says. "I see that before you left school, you were taking Grade Eleven English, Biology, Math, and Business."

I nod.

"Those are heavy courses," she says. "And trying to pick them all up again in the regular program might be a bit difficult. So, I'd like to connect you with Mr. Finnegan."

Have I heard that name before? "You want to connect me with *who*?" I ask.

"Mr. Finnegan," she says. "He's the teacher who's in charge of the alternative program here."

"'Alternative program'? I don't get it," I say. "How come I never heard about it?"

"It's quite a small program at the far wing of the school. Students in the program usually do their classes online," Mrs. Tang says. "Mr. Finnegan is there to help you if you run into difficulty. Nobody is directly teaching you. Each student works on their own computer, learning the course material at their own speed."

"So no actual teachers and no actual classes?"

"That's right," Mrs. Tang says.

This could work after all.

"In addition to doing your online lessons," Mrs. Tang continues, "you would have to participate in counselling."

There's the catch!

"I'd have to talk about my problems and stuff in front of a group?" That thought makes me cringe.

"Of course, nobody can make you talk if you don't wish to." Mrs. Tang gives me a crooked smile. "But you are required to attend the group sessions — even if you don't choose to speak up right away."

"Or at all?"

She doesn't answer me. "Your aunt tells me you are recovering from some physical trauma. Plus, you've had some recent family upheaval. So starting with one or two subjects at a time might be a good idea. You and Mr. Finnegan can chat about that," she says, "assuming you'd like to try going that route."

It doesn't look like I have any other choice.

Chapter 6

Despite The Odds

Up ahead, the words 'DESPITE THE ODDS' are painted in big, blue letters on the wall. Some other words are painted around it. *Success. Hurdle. Overcome. Pride. Achieve.*

"The DTO program is in this wing of the school," Mrs. Tang says. "DTO stands for 'despite the odds.' It's for students who have had some challenges in their lives. Many of them need a more flexible program in order to finish high school. We want them to be successful despite whatever challenges they're facing."

As we step through the doors, the school cop is leaving. He started coming to our school at the start of the semester — just before Rob kicked me out.

"Constable Haddad," Mrs. Tang begins, "this is a new student —"

I don't wait for her to finish. I lower my head and walk faster. From what I've learned, cops are never in the right place at the right time. Like, where was a cop when the guy was kicking the crap out of me under the bridge?

When I get to the end of the hall, I pause to let Mrs. Tang catch up. We step inside the classroom together. Sure enough, everyone is working at their own computer wearing their own headset. The group includes a pregnant-looking goth girl, a guy with a full-sleeve tattoo, a frail-looking girl with eyes darting everywhere, and a few others. Some of them glance up at me, but that's all. Nobody is talking and no awkward sharing sessions are going on. So far, so good.

"Finn," Mrs. Tang says, "I have someone here for you to meet."

A stocky man wearing jeans and a plaid shirt stands up from behind a desk. I take in his shaved head, his reddish-grey beard, and the small, gold hoop in one ear.

"This is Zaine," Mrs. Tang says. "It looks like he's going to be your new student."

"Welcome to the DTO classroom, Zaine," Mr. Finnegan says. "This is where we turn student hardships into success stories. *Despite* what's been going on in their personal lives."

Okay, so that just sounded totally lame.

Mrs. Tang checks the time. "Zaine, I'm going to leave you here with Mr. Finnegan. I need to return to my office to make a call. Any time you want to chat, my door is always open."

"Sure thing," Mr. Finnegan says. "I'm happy to take over." Then he turns to me. "First of all, we keep things pretty casual here. You can call me 'Mr. Finnegan' if you like. But I'm not exactly a teacher. I'm more like a coach. Most of the students just call me Finn. It's your call though."

I nod my head. It'd be easier if he just told me what he wanted me to call him.

He points toward the two rows of computers. "These are the students' work stations." Then he walks me over to a carpeted area beneath the windows. "And this is where we have our group talks every morning."

I assume he means the counselling sessions. Maybe the comfy-looking couches and cozy chairs are supposed to put students at ease so they'll open up about their problems. That won't be happening for me. I walk across the grey rug without saying a word.

As Finn leads me over to an empty computer, I realize I've been holding my breath. Aside from the twins with their millions of questions, I'm not really used to talking to anyone. I need to hurry things along.

"Mrs. Tang said I could start with just one or two subjects," I say. "I'm thinking Grade Eleven Biology and maybe Business. Bio was going okay until —"

I catch myself. I can't have Finn thinking that I'm the sharing type.

"— until I missed some school," I finish.

Finn nods and turns on a computer at the end of the first row. "This can be your work space, okay?"

I look around me. There's an empty computer between me and the pregnant goth girl. This is probably as good as it's going to get.

"Sure."

Finn uses a swipe card to log me in. Then he opens the online Bio program. "Let's start with this. The first unit is 'Energy and Matter Exchange in the Biosphere.'"

I scan down the screen. "I remember some of the stuff about food chains and food webs," I say.

"Well, you were only here for the start of the term," Finn says. "You might want to just redo it. There's a quiz at the end of each lesson. If you get seventy-five per cent or more, you can move on to the next lesson. Then there's a bigger test at the end of each unit."

My mind is stuck on the part about needing to get seventy-five per cent. I've never got that in my life. This will take me forever!

Finn leaves and I start reading the first lesson about photosynthesis. I'm partway through when the door bangs open. A guy in a wheelchair with a massive scowl pushes his way into the room. A backpack and a coat are laid across his lap.

"I already told you — I don't want your help!" he yells behind him. The door bangs shut a moment later.

I glance at the others. Goth Girl is totally ignoring him. Same with Tattoo Artist. Other than Shy Girl, who shrinks lower into her chair, nobody looks surprised. Maybe this happens all the time.

The guy in the wheelchair rolls up to a computer that's sitting on a lower desk. He slides his chair beneath it. He runs his hands through his messy brown hair, then he pulls on his glasses.

"Hey, Lucas," Finn calls over. "I can come help you out in a minute."

The whole time, Lucas is swearing and muttering to himself.

I'm closer to him than I want to be. His temper along with *my* temper might not be a great combination. And even with the headset on, it would be a lot easier to read if Lucas wasn't complaining to Finn about his wheelchair. Sure, it looks like the guy has it rough, but who doesn't?

"Don't beat yourself up." Finn is kneeling beside him. "You'll be out of the wheelchair soon. You need to be more patient with yourself."

"Easy for you to say!" Then Lucas notices me looking his way. "What are you looking at?"

"Not much." I glare back at him. "Just some whiner who needs to shut the hell up."

Goth Girl chuckles beside me. Maybe I'm not the only one who who's sick of him.

Lucas's face is bright red as he reaches across his desk for his glasses case. He whips it at me. I catch it in an awkward grab just before it smacks me in the face.

Before I know it, I'm on my feet. My chair clatters against the grey tile floor. Finn jumps to his feet as well. He's faster than I thought and he's pushing me back. I get the feeling he's done this before.

"Go sit down, Zaine." His teeth are clenched. "That's not how things work in this classroom."

I slam Lucas's glasses case onto the floor. Even though it's empty, it still feels good to have thrown something. I stomp back to my desk.

Finn goes back to talking with Lucas. "Your leg is still healing," he says. "So you might as well polish off a few more math lessons at the same time. No one will thank you if you don't, right?"

That sounds like a load of crap to me.
I'm surprised that Lucas actually shuts up and
starts doing his work. Before long, Constable
Haddad steps back into the room. He seems
to be a regular. I guess he's supposed to be the
big-brother type who's here to keep everyone on
their best behaviour.

Good luck with that, Constable Haddad.

I glance at the carpeted area. One thing
for sure is that I won't be sharing anything over
there. Or anywhere else, for that matter. Thank
god I've missed today's group session. That
gives me until tomorrow to figure out a way to
get out of it.

Chapter 7

Classmates

The locker that was assigned to me is in the main section of the high school, not the wing where DTO is. Now that I've been back at school for a week, I've seen some students coming and going who I recognize. None of them are exactly my friends, which is fine by me. I have zero interest in making friends, especially because I don't know how long I'll be here. Aunt Sarah still hasn't said whether she's going to throw me out or not.

I'm surprised that Bio is going better than I thought. I've just finished the lesson on aquatic life when Finn calls everyone over to the carpet. Or to use his word, he *invites* us to go there. I learned earlier this week that saying 'no' to his invitation is not an option.

We've all sat down on the chairs and couches when Constable Haddad lumbers into the room. His knees almost hit his shoulders when he drops down onto a stool beside the carpet. I'm sure it's no accident that he happened by just as the group session was starting. He smiles widely. The chip in his front tooth is visible as he looks around the circle. Meanwhile, all I can think of is how I don't trust the guy. I've also been avoiding Lucas as much as I can. I haven't even looked at him since my first day here.

"Let's go around the circle and hear from everyone," Finn says. "Remember, you can keep it simple. Just tell anything about what's going on in your life. Anything that the group might be able to offer some insights into."

I think he directs that last part toward Lucas and me. We're the only ones who never share anything.

The goth girl, Nina, looks up and shifts on the couch. Finn's head immediately swivels toward her.

"Nina, maybe you'd like to begin."

"Okay," Nina says. "So, as everyone can see, I'm kinda pregnant, right?"

I can hardly believe nobody shouts out *No shit!*

"It's getting harder to face all the other students," Nina continues. "Like, with me growing to the size of a Coke machine. And whenever the alien-child moves, it feels like a complete bounce across my bladder. Any idea what it's like having your bladder used for a trampoline?"

Afraid not, Nina. But I recently got kicked in that general area. Does that count?

I mostly tune her out as she talks about maybe having to drop out of school. When I finally glance up again, Finn has moved on to his next counselling victim, the shy mouse girl. Her name is 'Legacy.' Maybe that's where her problems started. Even though Mom could easily win the Least Responsible Parent Award, she at least didn't give me a lame-ass name like that.

In a tiny, pinched voice, Legacy describes how hard it is choosing her clothes each day. She also needs a lot of time to arrange her bedroom 'just so' before she leaves for school.

"And then, all the sounds and smells and people on the city bus freak me out," she says. "I'm exhausted by the time I get to school."

Slater, or Tattoo Artist, describes his deadbeat dad and his mom with the addiction problems. "My family is still as messed-up as ever," he says.

Join the club, Slater.

"And life didn't get any better," he says, "when we discovered I was VLT-positive."

"Um, don't you mean '*HIV*-positive?'" Nina asks.

"No, *VLT*-positive." Slater scratches his arm, just above the python tattoo. "VLTs are 'video-lottery terminals,'" Slater says. "Machines where you sit and gamble. I've been spending a lot of time — and money — at them. I like them a bit too much. So that's me." Slater points to himself. "Mr. VLT-positive."

I tune Slater back out again. Constable Haddad soon mutters something about having another appointment to go to. He gets up and leaves. I wish I could do the same thing.

I swear the clock has hardly moved as we turn next to Yvette. She swishes her long curls back from her face. Then she starts in about having to raise her little sisters all by herself.

"*Maman* died three years ago," she says. "And *Papa* has been too out of the picture to help out."

"What do you mean by 'out of the picture?'" Slater asks. "Like, sleeping it off?"

"No," Yvette says. "In jail."

After that, I nod off for a bit. Nina gives

me a nudge as Astrid, the red-haired girl, talks about getting expelled from her old school for cyberbullying. I wonder what genius decided it was a good idea for Astrid the Cyber Bully to spend her days behind a computer.

We've almost finished going around the circle when Lucas stands up. It looks like he's about to do some sharing. That totally pisses me off. That means I'm the only one who isn't spilling my guts. I wouldn't put it past him to talk just to try to make me look bad.

Then I notice something.

Oh my god!

As he adjusts the crutches under his armpits, I realize the bottom part of his right leg is missing. Up until now, he's always had his legs covered up with a jacket or blanket or something and he's usually been in his wheelchair. *Shit!* I can't believe I nearly got into a fight with a guy who only has one full leg.

Lucas notices people watching him. "I'm just going to take a leak, okay?"

From where I'm sitting, I can see something that the rest of the group can't. Lucas's face has turned a sickly shade of grey. He's swaying on his crutches like he's about to pass out.

I dash over and make a grab for him, but I'm too late. As he collapses at my feet, he yells out a string of swears. And he's directing all those F-bombs at me. After I just tried to help him!

Finn rushes over. "Let's untangle you." He shifts Lucas enough to pull his crutches out from under him. Then he helps Lucas onto the couch.

"Let's have everyone return to their work stations now," Finn says. "And thanks for trying to help, Zaine."

I glance over to see if Lucas picked up on that. That I was actually trying to help him. Jeez, I won't make that mistake again.

Lucas's face is extra pale and his eyelids are fluttering. Still, he complains when Finn calls his house to get someone to come pick him up.

"He seems better now," Finn says into the phone. "But he had a weak spell in class and he fell. I know he hates his wheelchair. But maybe it's too soon for him to come to school with just his crutches."

Finn turns to Lucas. "Your grandfather will be here as soon as he can."

When Lucas's grandfather finally shows up, he's pushing a wheelchair. I think the wheelchair is for Lucas, but it looks like the old man could use one too. He's also on crutches.

"Oh no!" Finn says. "I didn't realize you had an accident yourself. I'm sorry I had to disturb you. The fall happened fast. Zaine," he nods toward me, "tried to grab Lucas before he fell."

Lucas's grandfather turns around. For the first time, I see his face.

Then I realize this isn't the first time I've seen it at all. The old guy realizes it too.

"That kid!" he points at me. "I want him arrested. Now!"

Chapter 8

Busted

That gravelly voice has yelled in my head dozens of times since the night Mom bailed on me and I broke into the shed. All over again, I remember that guy's boozy breath on me and his flashlight shining in my face. I'm sure he got a good look at me.

Finn is instantly beside me. "Do you know what Lucas's grandfather is talking about?"

I open my mouth but no words come out. I just nod my head. Finn stares at me for a moment, then turns toward the class. "Everyone's going home a bit early today," he says. "See you tomorrow."

Their eyes are on me as they leave. Meanwhile, the old guy's face is bright red as he sputters about his broken ankle and what he thinks of young punks like me. My gut is telling me to run. But that would be pointless — just like trying to deny that I was the kid who broke into his shed.

Finn grabs his phone from his desk. "Is Constable Haddad still in the school?" He pauses for a moment. "No? And he isn't coming back here today?"

Finn has to yell into the phone to try to speak over top of the old guy.

". . . and as a veteran with twenty-five years of military service, I deserve to be treated with a bit of respect!" When he finally stops ranting, it's only long enough to pull out his cell phone. I know exactly who he's calling. The cops.

Lucas shifts on the couch. I don't know what to make of the stony look on his face. I can't sit still any longer. I'm pacing at the back of the room when two cops arrive.

As soon as they set foot in the room, the old guy — Mr. Wilkie K. Giezenman, as he keeps repeating — starts filling them in about me breaking into his shed. He goes on forever about how I made him break his ankle. That pisses me off. I sure as hell never told him to play the hero and chase me through the ravine.

"If you ask me," he continues, "young punks like that need to be locked up. Then maybe honest citizens can feel safe in their own homes." He nods at Lucas on the couch. "And this while I'm keeping care of my grandson."

"Did you file a report at the time?" one of the cops asks him.

"No, I didn't file no damn report," he says.

"You'll need to go downtown to the station to do that," the cop says. He motions at Lucas. "Are you okay to take this young man home first?"

"Of course I am," the old guy sputters. "No thanks to that little punk!"

Once he gets Lucas settled into the wheelchair, he takes off out the door. He has to partly lean on the wheelchair while Lucas holds on to both their crutches. At least I get a break from listening to him ranting.

That's the only upside though. The other cop is peppering me with questions. My name, any gang involvement, and finally —

"Where are your parents, Zaine?"

I glance at the name on her badge. I don't know how to answer Constable Persaud about my missing-in-action mom. It's the same with my father, the Japanese mystery man who Mom dated for a few months.

"I live with my aunt," I finally answer. I give her Aunt Sarah's name and phone number.

Constable Persaud is trying to reach Aunt Sarah but she's not getting through. I keep hoping Aunt Sarah is out somewhere with the twins, like maybe playing at the park.

Anywhere — just so she's not at home to get that call from the cops.

Constable Persaud finally turns to Finn. "So this young man is your student?"

"Yes, that's right."

"I can't reach his aunt," she says. "Are you available to come down to the police station with him instead?"

"Um, sure."

It's pretty decent of Finn to join me. I'm sure he never planned to spend his afternoon riding downtown in the grubby backseat of a cop car. Neither did I, come to think of it. I scuff my feet across the gravel on the floor mats, keeping my face down the whole time.

We get to the police station sooner than I hoped. Our timing is lousy too. Just as we step into the orange brick building, Mr. Giezenman is on his way out. At least Lucas isn't with him.

"You!" He stabs his gnarled old index finger toward me. "I'd like to see you haul your butt over to my place and repair the damage you caused." He pauses to adjust his crutches. "You've got no respect for other people and their property. Do you, you little smartass!"

For the second time today, everyone is looking at me. The old guy goes on and on about how his cast screws everything up. About him being fit and active all his life — up until now. And about him being a military veteran and a retired boxer.

A *boxer*? Jeez. I was luckier than I knew getting away from him that night.

"Once I get this cast off," he says, "you're welcome to pull on the gloves and step into the ring with me. I'd be happy to teach you a lesson or two."

It's only then that Constable Persaud tells him to settle down. "You've made your report," she says. "Now it's time for you to leave."

The old guy sucks in his breath with a loud snort. He's still sputtering when Constable Persaud leads Finn and me down the hall. The room she takes us into has grey walls and a cold tile floor. An 'interview room,' she calls it.

A chill has gripped my whole body. I can't stop shivering as I drop onto the hard metal chair closest to the door. Finn pulls up a chair beside me. From the corner of my eye, I can see his eyelid twitching. Maybe I'm the first of his students to ever get arrested.

"See that camera?" Constable Persaud points. "The rest of our conversation will be videotaped. That's to make sure we've followed all the necessary steps."

Next, she starts reading me my rights. I hope Finn is listening, because my brain has totally shut down. I just barely catch the part about my right to have a lawyer present.

Constable Persaud points toward a phone and a phone book. "Go ahead," she says. "Make some calls."

Chapter 9

Two Weeks

A sign taped onto the wall has the number for a 24-hour phone line to Legal Aid. I think 'legal aid' means that it's free. Aunt Sarah doesn't have much money so that's probably who I need to call. But all I can think about is what she's going to do when she finds out about this. The police haven't been able to reach her yet. That feels like the only thing that's gone right so far. That's also why I need to move this forward.

So, when Constable Persaud asks me what I did and why I did it, I tell her everything. I can't wait for a lawyer to show up. I can barely say it in front of Finn. There's no way I could do it if Aunt Sarah was here. I've got to get it over with.

My voice is totally flat as I describe being really mad when I finally got inside the shed. That I never went there to wreck the shed. That I didn't mean for the old guy to get hurt. I'm sweating and shivering in turns. When I've finished, Constable Persaud leaves the room.

After what feels like hours, the door to the interview room opens. Constable Persaud steps inside with Aunt Sarah. I shrink when her eyes land on me.

It takes me a few tries before I can get any words out. "Um, where are the twins?"

"I dropped them off next door." Aunt Sarah is staring right into me. I get the feeling she doesn't like what she sees. I can't believe that a week ago, I thought my life was improving. That Mom was coming back and that we'd be moving back in together. Instead —

"Zaine Alexander Wyatt," Constable Persaud says. "You are charged with break and enter to commit the indictable offence of mischief. And break and enter to commit the indictable offence of theft. You are also charged with assault causing bodily harm."

I struggle to take everything in. The charges, plus a court appearance in seven weeks.

"In the meantime," Constable Persaud goes on, "you are to have no contact with the complainant, Mr. Giezenman. You also cannot approach Mr. Giezenman's premises. Your curfew is nine o'clock p.m. both on weekdays and on weekends. If it's necessary to be out later than that, you must be accompanied by your guardian, Sarah Wyatt. We will also assign you a probation officer to report to. This is to ensure you are abiding by these conditions."

Constable Persaud turns to Finn. "You can go home now," she says. "That's everything we need from you, too, Zaine."

"So, I'm done?" I ask.

"For tonight only." She leans toward me. "Young man, this is far from over."

Her eyes are still drilling into me as I leave the station. We step outside and Aunt Sarah comes to a sudden stop. I nearly crash into her.

"Zaine, it's one thing to get in trouble at school," she says. "And now you're in trouble with the police, too?" Her voice is growing higher. "I need you to tell me this one thing — and don't you dare lie to me. Did you do these terrible things the police charged you with?"

My voice completely seizes up. All I can do is nod.

"God, Zaine!" Tears are forming in her eyes. "You actually think it's okay to break into an old man's shed and assault him?"

I want to tell her it didn't happen like that but —

"How can this have happened?" Her shoulders shake as she starts to cry. "My marriage has just crumbled around me. I have two children to raise on my own. And now this?"

All down the sidewalk, people are staring at us.

"It's like you haven't learned *anything* about how to be a decent human being." She dashes away some tears as I shuffle from one foot to the other.

The worst part is that I agree with her. Even though I've tried, I'm no better than a street cat. Like the ones with torn ears and battered tails that I would hear fighting in the alleys when I was walking the streets all those cold, horrible nights. "You've left me with no choice, Zaine." Aunt Sarah takes a deep, ragged breath. "You have two weeks to find another place to live. Then you need to leave."

Despite the warm day, my blood freezes. I have no family or friends I can move in with. So it's back out onto the streets.

Suddenly, my mind flashes back to the guy who attacked me under the bridge. I wonder what *his* life has been like. How many times has he been beaten up? And what if that's who I turn into after a few more years and a few more beatings?

Aunt Sarah's words cut into my thoughts. "As soon as I can reach your mom," she says, "I'll tell her. As it is . . ." Aunt Sarah's voice trails off.

Mom. If she hears about me getting charged by the police, she won't *ever* want me living with her again. I can't decide if it's a good thing or a bad thing that we lost touch with her since she moved in with her 'special guy.' And is there any point in me working ahead in my Bio class?

After how today has gone, I feel like the creature on the bottom of the food chain. The one that's most likely to get eaten alive by predators. That's pretty much what life was like on the streets — where I'll be returning in two weeks.

Chapter 10

Fletch and the Clones

After everything that happened yesterday, I was awake most of the night. Then I slept in this morning. I'm not looking forward to going back to school, but I'm also afraid of what might happen if I skip.

Everyone looks up when I skid into class late. Then they quickly look back down again at their screens. Lucas mutters something as I walk by. His glasses case is sitting on his desk, at least until he decides to pitch it at me again.

I pull up in front of my computer and try to tune out all the crap that's running through my head. I've finished working on the exchange of energy in the biosphere. I might as well take the test. If nothing else, this might take my mind off of heading back out on the streets again.

The first part of the test goes okay. I know the answers to these questions. But then I have to guess on some of the next ones. I'm sweating by the time I finish the whole thing. Then I sit back in my chair while the computer scores my test.

While I'm waiting, I look around the room. Nina looks even more pregnant than she did yesterday. When Legacy sees me looking at her, she jumps. Yvette's head is bobbing like she's ready to fall asleep at her computer. None of us look well-rested today.

Just then, a *ping* interrupts my thoughts. I look back down at my computer. My eyes nearly pop. Seventy-eight per cent!

Any other time, I'd want to tell Aunt

Sarah right away. But I'll probably be quitting school in two weeks anyway. I doubt that even the DTO program is flexible enough to work around my upcoming life on the streets. The excitement I felt at getting my first-ever grade of seventy-eight seems cruel.

The classroom door opens and Constable Haddad appears. I duck my head and try to look busy. It doesn't work though.

"Zaine," he says, "Mrs. Tang and I would like to chat with you. Can you come with me to the main office?" He says it as though I actually have a choice.

Everyone's eyes follow me as I leave with him. We've just stepped out of the DTO wing when I see a guy I know. Fletch always had a tough-guy swagger. I also remember how he enjoyed bullying the weaker kids at school. Even with my anger issues, I would have guessed Fletch would be in trouble with the cops long before I was.

He always seemed like a loner, but today

he's sitting by an open locker with a couple buddies. They look like clones in their baggy jeans, black T-shirts and ball caps screwed backward onto their heads. They even have the same sneers on their faces.

As we make our way down the hall, Fletch does an exaggerated sniff. "God, this hallway reeks. It smells like *pigs*!"

His two clones start laughing like it's the funniest thing ever.

"Hey, Zaine," Fletch calls. "Keep an eye out for pigs, okay?"

Constable Haddad grits his teeth and keeps walking.

"Wait out here," he says when we get to the office. "I need to talk to Mrs. Tang first."

While he's inside with her, I check out the Cambodian flag. Mrs. Tang must have just hung that on her door this week. For the third time, I'm re-reading about the *riel* they use for money in Cambodia, and the facts about the massive Angkor Wat temple. My knee bounces while I'm sitting in the hard chair.

Mrs. Tang opens the door, and I try to look casual. She sets her red cat-eye glasses among the spikes of her black hair and motions me inside. "Zaine, Constable Haddad heard from his colleague that you were at the police station yesterday."

I figured word would get around fast. I don't know if she's waiting for an answer from me, so I just sit still and keep my mouth shut.

"I think I might be able to help you, Zaine," Constable Haddad says.

Help me? I doubt it — unless he's planning to adopt an at-risk teen.

"Have you ever heard of restorative justice?" Constable Haddad asks.

I shake my head.

"I recently took some training in it," he says. "Restorative justice is a circle process where we talk about what happened. If Mr. Giezenman agrees, we can meet with him in a group."

It's bad enough that I have to see his grandson every day.

"It's an opportunity to discuss how he was affected by your actions. And how you might repair the harm you caused him."

How do you repair a broken ankle?

"It also might be possible for you to avoid a criminal record."

Hey, maybe Aunt Sarah won't throw me out after all!

"I understand that you've been charged with break and enter, mischief, theft, and assault causing bodily harm. Your actions led to Mr. Giezenman getting injured. You also caused considerable damage to his property. Isn't that so?"

"Yeah." I keep my eyes down on my running shoes.

"First of all," Constable Haddad says, "I'm going to contact Mr. Giezenman. If he agrees to address the matter using this process, I'll schedule our meeting. You'll be brought face-to-face with him at a meeting called a restorative circle."

"I don't get it. What would I have to —"

"You would then have to do whatever the group decides on to make up for the harm you've caused. And a few more questions," Constable Haddad continues. "I understand you live with your aunt?"

"Yeah." *For now.*

"Do we need to advise your parents as well?"

"No," I say. *As if.*

Constable Haddad is writing everything down. "I've spoken with Constable Persaud. I told her not to assign you a probation officer. Since I'm here at the school anyway, I'll do the regular check-ins with you myself. And you remember about your curfew, right?"

"Yeah."

"One last thing," Constable Haddad says. "Even though you'll have support throughout this process, it might be the hardest thing you've ever done."

The hardest thing I've ever done? Really? I think about Mom ditching me four years ago. About living on the street and having to fight to survive. About getting beaten up under the bridge. And about Aunt Sarah planning to throw me out of the house again soon.

And Constable Haddad thinks this will be harder? I seriously doubt that.

I decide to keep my mouth shut. I just nod my head and hope this restorative thing saves my ass after all.

Chapter 11

Face-To-Face

Fletch and his friends are often hanging out near my locker when I get to school. They disappear pretty fast when Constable Haddad comes to check in with me there. That's kind of too bad. Maybe having some friends would be okay. It might even give me someone to lean on when Aunt Sarah boots me out of the house again.

Because I'm still showing up for class, I need to sit in on the sessions around the carpet.

Today, Nina is talking more about trying to finish her English credit before "the alien goth baby" arrives. Legacy is still struggling to leave the house each day. As usual, I tune out most of it until Finn lets us go back to our computers.

Finn soon drops into the empty chair beside me. "Zaine, I have some good news," he says. "Constable Haddad says that Mr. Giezenman has agreed to restorative justice. They've scheduled a meeting for Saturday morning."

Saturday morning. That's one of my last days at Aunt Sarah's place — unless she changes her mind about kicking me out.

"It starts at nine o'clock sharp," Finn continues. "It'll be here at school, in the staffroom." He checks a note on his phone. "Constable Haddad has confirmed that the date works for Mr. Giezenman, and for your mom, too."

Mom?

Finn looks at his notes more closely.

"Actually, it's Mr. Giezenman and your *aunt*."

Oh, thank god.

After Finn steps away, I try to practice what I'm going to say to Aunt Sarah about the meeting. I'm not looking forward to that conversation. But I hope I can convince her not to kick me out.

When I get home from school, Aunt Sarah is watching a cooking show on TV. Carter and Lawson have taken the cushions off the couch to build pillow forts.

Aunt Sarah speaks up first. "Zaine, did your teacher talk to you about the meeting on Saturday morning?"

"Yeah." Then I lower my voice so the twins can't hear. "Uh, does that mean I can keep living here?"

Aunt Sarah's lips are set in a tight line. "I'll wait to hear what everyone has to say before I decide."

At least it wasn't a 'no.' Still, I was hoping she'd just agree.

***

My stomach is in knots as we walk to the
meeting.

"It's almost nine o'clock," Aunt Sarah says.
"We need to hurry."

When we get to the school, I follow Aunt
Sarah into the staffroom. Constable Haddad
— who probably sleeps in his uniform — is
perched on a chair that is way too small for
him. An older, beefy-looking guy who looks
like he might have played pro football when
he was younger is beside him. Finn is here,
too. Aside from them, it's just Aunt Sarah and
me. There's no sign of Mr. Giezenman who,
for obvious reasons, I've come to think of as
'Geezer.'

While I wait, I look around the staffroom.
The ancient-looking stove with the stained
burners. The year-long calendar on the
wall with exams, assemblies, and PD Days
written on it. The notice board with student

suspensions listed below. I'm sure my name has appeared there in the past.

Suddenly, something falls onto the floor out in the hallway. Some swears follow. Constable Haddad dashes from the room.

"Can I help you with that?" he asks. "I've got the damn thing myself!" There's no mistaking *that* voice.

When Mr. Giezenman appears, he fires me a glare. Then he bumps down into a seat. Constable Haddad folds himself back into his chair.

"Is anyone else joining you today, Mr. Giezenman?" Constable Haddad asks.

"Like my grandson?" Geezer says. "No, he's not coming. Lucas doesn't give a shit what happens to this kid." He shoots me another killer glare. "Can't say as I blame him."

Great. What a perfect start.

"Okay then," Constable Haddad says. "First of all, I'd like to thank everyone for coming to discuss the break-in that occurred at Mr. Giezenman's shed. Zaine is here to take responsibility for it. He also wishes to find ways to make amends for the harm he caused."

Constable Haddad does a round of introductions. It turns out that Football Guy is Constable Haddad's instructor for the restorative-justice training he just took.

"As you are all aware," Constable Haddad says, "Zaine Wyatt entered onto property belonging to Mr. Wilkie Giezenman on the evening of March twenty-ninth. When Mr. Giezenman went to investigate, he came upon Zaine, who had forcibly entered the shed.

"While inside the shed, Zaine caused extensive damages. A struggle ensued and Mr. Giezenman pursued Zaine from his property. He suffered a broken ankle when he was hit by the wrench that Zaine threw. As a result of this incident, Zaine has been charged with the following offences —"

I do my best to tune him out. I don't need to hear those charges all over again. Sweat is streaming down my forehead.

Drip. Drip.

"We're going to talk about how this has affected everyone," Constable Haddad says. "We'll then discuss what we would like to see happen to repair the damage. Zaine, let's begin with you."

Oh no! I didn't know I'd have to go first! I thought I'd get to hear everyone else. Then I'd figure out what to say.

"Go back to when this began for you, Zaine," Constable Haddad says. "Just tell us from start to finish."

Drip. Drip.

The problem is, I don't know where this actually began. Was it when Mom ditched me four years ago? Or did it start when I stormed out of Aunt Sarah's house that night? Since I'm not ready to talk about Mom ditching me, I decide to jump in around the middle.

"I know this looks really bad on me," I say. "And maybe nobody will believe me. But I didn't mean for any of this to happen. I especially didn't mean for Mr. Giezenman to get hurt."

Drip. Drip.

"That garden shed used to be someone's art studio," I say. "I used to go there to cool off whenever Rob, Aunt Sarah's husband, was giving me a hard time." I run my sweaty palms up and down the front of my jeans. "So I went back to the shed that night because I was really mad. I thought that being there would stop me from exploding and from doing something stupid. I didn't know it belonged to someone new."

There. Hopefully I've told them enough.

I glance around the room. I can tell by the looks on their faces that they're waiting for me to offer them more. But the pressure inside me is building. I'm gripping the sides of the chair. I need to finish this off before I totally lose it.

"So the reason I got really mad," I say, "is that my mom ditched me. She's the only family I have. When she left town, she said it would be for just a few months. But it's been four years.

Since then, I've lived with Aunt Sarah. And when Rob kicked me out a while back, I lived on the streets for three weeks — until I got beat up really bad."

I hear a choking sound beside me. It's Aunt Sarah. I can't look at her crying. I just need to get this over with.

"Mom promised that she was finally coming back to Melton Grove and getting a place for us," I say. "I really thought she was going to do it. But then she phoned and said she wasn't."

My voice catches from somewhere deep down in my chest. My breath is all raspy and bumpy. Tears are streaming down my cheeks. I swipe my arm across my face.

"That's what was going on the night I broke into Mr. Giezenman's shed." I take a few deep breaths. Then I remember something else. "And, about the wrench —"

"Yeah," Geezer says. "I remember the wrench all too well."

"When I threw the wrench," I say, "I wasn't trying to hit you. You were chasing me and I forgot I was still holding it. I just meant to throw the wrench away so I could run faster. But then it hit you."

I sit back into my chair. I look around the room trying to gauge everyone's reaction. More than anything, I need to get out of this. I can't wind up back on the streets.

Then I think of something else to say. Something that they seem to be waiting for. "And I'm really sorry." I hope that sounded sincere.

"Thanks, Zaine," Constable Haddad says.

He doesn't look like he's expecting me to say anything else. Thank god for that. Someone else can do the talking now.

Chapter 12

Damages

"Next, we'll turn to Mr. Giezenman," Constable Haddad says. "Can you tell us what happened the night of March twenty-ninth?"

I'm not surprised when Geezer goes into great detail about everything. About the crashing he heard in his shed and about going to check it out.

"And here," he says, "is the damage this young punk did." Geezer pulls some papers out of his pocket. It takes him about a year and a half to unfold them before he starts reading. "One bicycle: ruined. One punching bag: torn apart. Fourteen flower pots: smashed all to hell. Two pairs of . . ."

I'm probably not the only one who tunes him out.

". . . shin pads: torn. And lastly, one windowpane: shattered." Geezer looks around the room. "But you know what galls me most of all? That he didn't take responsibility for what he did right away. Instead, he pushed me out of the way. Then he chucked a wrench at me. Now I'm stuck with this —" he taps his crutch against the cast "— for another five weeks. And the timing couldn't be worse. I have a family obligation to see to."

A family obligation? Lucas?

"Would you like to explain about that family obligation?" Constable Haddad asks.

"Nah." Geezer flaps his hand like he's shooing away a fly. "I'm done."

"Okay," Constable Haddad says. "Let's

hear next from Zaine's aunt. Sarah, what can you tell us?"

Aunt Sarah is fidgeting in her chair. "Zaine has lived with me for four years now. He's staying with me and my twin sons while my sister, Beth, is . . ."

I glance sideways at her. What exactly does Aunt Sarah think Mom is doing?

". . . while Beth is doing some travel and sorting out her life."

Aunt Sarah's lip quivers. "I don't believe Zaine meant to injure Mr. Giezenman. But he's getting in more and more trouble all the time. So when the police phoned to say Zaine was down at the station, I had to tell Zaine he can't live with his little cousins and me any longer. That he had two weeks to find another place to live."

A hush has fallen over the room. The only sound is Aunt Sarah crying.

Constable Haddad runs his hand through the dark bristles on his head. When he finally speaks again, his voice is soft. "Do you have anything else to add, Sarah?"

She shakes her head, a tangle of tissues clutched in her hand.

"We'll turn next to Finn," Constable Haddad says. "What are your thoughts about what happened?"

Finn wipes a trickle of sweat from his forehead. "I've only known Zaine for a few weeks," he says. "Although Zaine is guarded around the other students, he's working hard to complete his Grade Eleven Biology credit.

"And what happened with Mr. Giezenman," Finn says, "I wasn't completely surprised. Zaine has had an altercation with another student in my class. I know he has some anger issues. For the most part though, I don't think Zaine would try to harm anyone on purpose," Finn continues. "Plus, he's working hard at his studies. I'd like to see him engage more with his peers. Still, I think Zaine is capable of making all of us proud, including himself."

A wave of guilt washes over me. I don't think I deserve the nice things that Finn just said.

Constable Haddad pauses. "Thanks, everyone, for sharing your thoughts," he finally says. "I'd also like to point out that Zaine has apologized. Do you accept his apology, Mr. Giezenman?"

"So far," Geezer drawls out his words, "all I've seen is a kid who destroys whatever the hell he wants. Then runs away without owning up. I have no reason to believe his apology is worth accepting."

"Fair enough," Constable Haddad says. "So now let's try to decide what we'd like to see happen to make things right."

We start going around the circle. The group agrees that I'll have to clean up inside the shed and pay for a locksmith. I'll also have to repaint the doorframe.

Then Football Guy speaks up. "It's going to be hard for Mr. Giezenman to do his outdoor chores. Maybe Zaine could do those for him. Things like digging up Mr. Giezenman's vegetable garden or painting his fence."

Aunt Sarah slowly raises her hand. "After what Zaine did, maybe Mr. Giezenman doesn't feel safe having Zaine on his property. I certainly wouldn't."

Oh no! Did Aunt Sarah seriously just say that?

"I'm not afraid of a little punk like him," Mr. Giezenman sneers. "It'll do me good to see him hauling his arse around my place."

"We haven't fully addressed the day-to-day problems that Mr. Giezenman is suffering," Constable Haddad says. "He's on crutches at the moment. Plus he has a grandson whose leg was recently amputated. Lucas is using either crutches or a wheelchair to get himself around. So, I think we need to hear some more suggestions."

"How about locking him up and throwing away the key," Geezer says.

As the minutes drag on, that actually starts to sound okay.

Constable Haddad turns to Geezer. "What have you found hardest to do since you broke your ankle?"

"Everything!" Geezer waves his hands in the air. "Grocery shopping, cleaning the house, cooking dinner."

"Then those are the very tasks that Zaine needs to take on," Constable Haddad says.

"Really?" The word is out of my mouth before I can stop it.

"Absolutely." Constable Haddad frowns at me. "That's what it means to take full responsibility for the damages you caused."

"There's one more thing," Geezer says. "Ever since my grandson's surgery, I've been driving him to school in the morning. That's not such a big deal. But after I've hauled myself around on these damn crutches all day, picking up Lucas after school is a pain in the arse.

"So, when you're leaving your class — DTO

or Despite or whatever the hell it's called — you can get him back home on the bus. When you get to my place, I'll line up some other stuff for you to do."

What the hell? I have to deal with Lucas *and* be Geezer's personal maid service?

I look around the circle. Everyone else is nodding their heads. They seem to think this is the best idea ever. But the last time Lucas and I were face-to-face with each other, we were ready to beat the crap out of each other.

"I don't think this is going to work, Mr. Geezer — uh, Giezenman."

Judging from Geezer's squinty eye, he heard the 'geezer' part.

"Remember, Zaine," Constable Haddad says, "you're facing criminal charges. Your job here is to convince me and the rest of the group that you're serious about making amends for the harm you've caused."

My face flushes and I sink further into my chair. After feeling like one of those bugs from science class with its guts all splayed out for everyone to gawk at, I agree just so I can go home.

"Mr. Giezenman said he'll be wearing the cast for another five weeks," Constable Haddad says. "So, Zaine, you are going to help him out for the next five weeks. One and a half hours after school each day seems reasonable to me.

"Then we will hold a final meeting to determine whether you have fulfilled the terms of the agreement. This will help me decide whether I feel justified in asking the Court to dismiss the charges against you."

"Hang on," I say. "Don't they *have* to drop the charges if I do all that stuff?"

"They're not required to," Constable Haddad says. "They could still uphold the charges."

"*What?*"

"They generally drop the charges," Constable Haddad continues, "as long as the person in question follows through on the agreement and shows remorse for their behaviour."

Football Guy leans over and whispers something to Constable Haddad.

"Oh yes," Constable Haddad says. "Sarah, you said that you plan to send Zaine out of your house because of the charges he's facing. Is that still the case?"

I freeze in my chair. This is what it comes down to right here.

"If Zaine does everything that we've decided on today," Aunt Sarah says, "he can keep living with me."

Oh, thank god!

"But only if the judge drops the charges," Aunt Sarah adds. "If Zaine breaks his probation or messes up in any way, he'll have to leave my home right away."

Chapter 13

Repairing The Harm

I'm used to Constable Haddad hanging out at my locker every morning to check in with me. He starts with the usual questions. *How's it going?* and *Did you have a good night last night?* But today, he looks more serious.

"Are you ready for your first meeting with Lucas and Mr. Giezenman?" he asks.

"Yeah. Sure." I try to sound casual.

"I know you and Lucas aren't exactly buddies. But this is important, Zaine."

Constable Haddad keeps his eyes locked onto mine. "You need to get him home from school without any fights or other problems. Then do whatever chores Mr. Giezenman tells you to. Don't mess around."

As Constable Haddad turns and walks down the hall, Fletch calls out to me. "Looks like you and the pig aren't seeing things eye to eye." He shakes his head. "Me, Skeeter, and Bryce — we knew as soon as the guy arrived at our school that he was on a power trip. What's he up to anyway?"

I toss my jean jacket into my locker and slam the door shut. "Just this thing I've gotta do," I say. "To get some charges dropped."

I didn't mean to say that last part. But I'm still rattled about starting to work with Geezer and Lucas today.

"Sounds like you've been busy." Fletch and the other two fall into step beside me.

While we walk down the hall together, it occurs to me that I'm finally doing what everyone else at school does. I'm hanging out with friends. I'm not completely sure these guys actually *are* my friends. Still, it feels okay for a change. And they seem to feel the same way I do about cops — especially about Constable Haddad.

I give them a wave as I step inside the classroom. Lucas looks the other way. I do the same. It's like we've both decided to ignore each other for the day. At least that's something we agree on.

After school, I'm reaching for Lucas's stuff to help load it into his backpack. "We have to hurry if we're gonna make the next bus," I say.

"Not so fast," Lucas says. "I'll decide what kind of help I want from you."

He shuffles his books and his glasses case and the rest of his crap. It takes forever for him to load up his backpack. By the time we leave the school, we've missed the first bus. I grit my teeth and pace around the bus stop while we wait for the next one.

When we finally get to Geezer's house, he hands me a massive list of jobs. Laundry. Scrubbing the bathroom. Cleaning the mouldy vegetables out of the fridge. He's wearing a walking cast now. He's not even using crutches any more. I'm sure he could do some of this stuff himself. Instead, he's ordering me around. The twisted, broken-nosed smile across his tough old face tells me he's enjoying every minute of it.

***

I've finished everything on the list when Geezer calls over to me. "You know how to cook?" He doesn't wait for me to answer. "Go scrub up," he says. "You're on for making dinner."

When I come back to the kitchen, he has pulled out some food onto the counter.

"You know how to make schnitzel?" he asks.

"I don't even know what that is," I say.

"Oh, for god's sake!" Geezer shakes his

head. "Over in that cupboard," he points. "Take out three bowls. You'll need them for dipping the meat into."

I'm trying to do what he asks. But he keeps sputtering and correcting me from the kitchen table. "Not like that! You dip the pork in the flour first. Then the egg. The bread crumbs are last.

"And get that frypan warming up," he says. "You think you can cook schnitzel in a cold skillet? Not friggin' likely!"

Just then, Lucas joins us in the kitchen. A scowl is fixed on his face. I can't believe I have five weeks of this to go. I clamp my jaw shut so I don't say anything.

When the schnitzel is golden-brown, I take it off the stove. I've also boiled some potatoes and carrots. It smells great. My stomach is grumbling as I walk out the door. I'm starving by the time I get to Aunt Sarah's house.

As soon as I step inside, the twins jump on me.

"Zaine!"

"Where you been?"

"I was helping someone out," I say.

"Why?" they ask.

"Because it's, um, my new job."

"Why?"

"Because the man and his grandson both hurt their legs."

"Why?"

I look over at Aunt Sarah. She smiles and shrugs. "How did everything go?"

"It was okay."

"That's good," Aunt Sarah says. "I saved your dinner in the fridge."

Carter speaks up. "Why do you —"

"No more questions right now," I say.

"Why?"

"Because I'm hungry enough to eat two kids named Carter and Lawson."

They squeal and run away. They're still giggling as I wolf down the leftover chicken and rice.

Chapter 14

The Squad

Over the next few weeks, Lucas and I still don't talk to each other while we're in class. That's fine with me. We're spending more than enough time together after school. Something else doesn't change. We're still the only two students who don't speak up during circle time at the carpet.

Today, Nina shifts again and again on the couch. "The countdown is on with the alien child," she says. "I got a feeling I need to finish this English credit soon."

It's my turn next. "Well, Nina," I say, "I'll help you get back to your schoolwork faster. Because guess what? I'm gonna pass."

"What?" Nina pretends she's surprised. "You're not gonna fill us in about your thrilling life?"

"No thanks," I say. "I'd hate to make everyone jealous."

That at least gets a laugh from the group.

Legacy is next. Just as I think she's going to pass too, she pipes up in her tiny, pinched voice. "I hardly made it to school today," she says. "I had to make my bed twelve times before I could leave the house. Lately, I've only had to make it eight times."

"Do you know why it was different today?" Finn asks.

Legacy nods. "My mom painted the hallway outside my bedroom. She's wanted to do it for a long time. I finally said she could. But the smell of the paint changed everything." She looks down at her feet. "So I needed to make my bed more times. Otherwise, it wouldn't be okay."

This is the most Legacy has ever said.

"And still, you made it here, Legacy," Finn says. "We're glad you did."

Then he turns to Lucas.

"Pass me," he says.

Slater speaks up next. "So, get this," he says. "I've been VLT-free for two weeks."

"No way," Astrid says. "So you're done with the gambling thing?"

"I wouldn't go that far," Slater says. "But two weeks is my longest stretch yet, so who knows."

Some of the students cheer. Slater tries to look cool about it. He can't fully pull it off though. Even the skull tattoo on his arm looks like it's blushing.

Yvette is up next. "I'm going to call my *Oncle Marcel*," she says. "Papa will be furious. He got into a big fight with my uncle years ago. They were both tanked. I bet neither one can even remember what the fight was about. But I need help. My little sisters are way too much work for me."

Once we've finished going around the circle, we all move back to our computers. At the end of the day when everyone starts trickling out of the class, I leave the room too. Over the past few weeks, I've learned that it's better if I wait for Lucas down the hall. That way I'm not apt to piss him off by trying to help him.

I'm stepping through the doors of the Despite wing when Fletch and the Clones see me.

"Zaine!" Fletch claps me across the shoulder.

"Oh, hey." I'm still trying to figure out what to think about these guys. It's kind of cool having people to hang with, even just for the few minutes before I have to leave with Lucas. But lately, I've been thinking that Fletch and the Clones seem like the kind of guys who could tip the balance for me. They're the kind of guys who could maybe get me sent back out onto the streets.

"We're heading downtown," Fletch says.

"Wanna join us?"

"I can't." I glance toward the classroom to see if Lucas is on his way out yet.

"You checking for the cripple?" Fletch asks.

The *cripple*? The hairs on the back of my neck bristle. "Um, Lucas?" I say. "Yeah."

"I think you need to improve on the company you're keeping these days." Fletch drawls out his words. "The cripple *and* the school cop? You can do better, man."

I swallow hard. "Yeah, maybe," I say. "But I got in a bit of trouble. Plus I spent some time on the streets. I didn't like it much." I shrug and try to look casual. "Now I've gotta help out around Lucas's place to make up for some damage I caused."

"Well, aren't you living the dream." Fletch screws his face up. "You know, you've got better options than that. Me and the boys here, we're joining the Squad real soon."

"A gang?"

"Yeah," Fletch says. "But it's more like a

brotherhood. Squad brothers look out for each other. Bet you coulda used *that* while you were on the street."

That much is true. I could have used some help from *anyone.*

"It doesn't look like things have been easy since you got off the street either." I nearly jump when I hear Skeeter's nasally voice. This is the first time I realized he could even speak. "Like, with that old guy on crutches ratting you out to the cops."

"Yeah," I say. "I could have done without that."

"He needs to show you some respect," Fletch says. "That's exactly what we'll be pulling in once we're full Squad members. Respect. We could put in a good word for you. And if you wanna get back at the old guy, we could all go break into his house. Have a bit of fun. Show him you won't put up with his shit. Take whatever is worth something. Whadya say?"

Oh man! My head is spinning. How did things take such a fast turn? I somehow don't think gang membership is what I need right now. And they want to break into Geezer and Lucas's house?

It takes me a few moments before I can answer. "Thanks for looking out for me, guys. But it's okay, you know?" I'm trying to sound calm. "I'm in enough trouble as it is."

"So you're turning us down?" Fletch says.

"Yeah," I say. "But thanks anyway."

I glance up the hall. What the hell is keeping Lucas? I need to get away from these guys.

"I've gotta go see what's up with Lucas," I say. "I'll see you around."

"Whatever, man," Fletch says. Then as I walk away, he adds, "I thought you had balls. But I guess not."

I grit my teeth as I walk back toward the classroom. A few weeks ago, I would have fought anyone who talked to me that way, even if I was outnumbered three to one. I'd have just let the rage carry me. But I've got to play it smarter. I don't have many chances left.

Chapter 15

"Shouldn't Take Long"

I try to shake off the conversation with Fletch and the Clones. But it's still ringing in my head when we get to Geezer's place.

Lucas is standing propped against the door frame with his crutches. We'd already be inside if he'd just give me the key. But over the last four weeks, I've learned to let him do it.

When we finally get inside, Geezer is pulled up on his brown leather easy chair. It looks almost as beaten-up as Geezer does. He snaps to attention when we walk through the door.

"Having a nap?" I ask.

"Hell, no." Geezer clears his throat. "I got no time for that."

Jeez. So taking a nap is a sign of weakness. It feels like time to change the subject. "Are you still getting that cast off next week?"

"Yeah," Geezer says. "About time."

"Cool. What do you need me to do today? More laundry? Vacuuming?" I ask as I tidy the shoes in the landing. "I bet you'll miss me here after this week. It must've been pretty sweet having your own personal servant." I say it carefully, with a smile on my face, so he knows I'm joking. Or at least, mostly joking.

"Yeah," Geezer grumbles. "All it cost me was a broken ankle and a trashed shed." He mumbles something else, too. I'm pretty sure he called me a 'little shithead.' But this time he didn't sound angry.

"You can start with bathroom detail," he says. "Shouldn't take long."

He always says that. *Shouldn't take long.* Even when a job *does* take long.

I give the mirrors a quick wipe down. Then I hold my breath and try not to gag while I clean the toilet. I slosh lots of Pine-Sol around the sink and the bathtub so the room smells fresh. Geezer doesn't exactly look that closely. That should do it.

Geezer watches me step out of the bathroom. "Done," I say.

"Good," he replies. "Now go back in and scrub up. You've got some more cooking to do."

At least that sounds better than toilet-brush duty.

"What am I making you today?" I ask.

"Scones," Geezer says. "You know — tea biscuits. To go with the leftover chicken stew."

"Oh. Okay." My main chore yesterday was making them chicken stew for dinner. "How was the stew?" I ask.

"It wasn't half bad." Geezer lifts himself out of his chair and stomps into the kitchen. He pulls out a splattered, ancient cookbook from a shelf.

"When you make scones," he says, "you need to use a light hand. Otherwise the biscuits end up so tough you could break a tooth on them."

Lucas comes into the kitchen too. He smiles while Geezer bosses me around about mixing the dry ingredients first. Then blending in the shortening. Then dumping the buttermilk in all at once.

"You don't mix it like that," Geezer says. "Remember what I said about a light hand? You're handling the dough too much."

"Then how do I get everything mixed together?" I shove the dough at him. "Here. You do it."

Geezer gives it a few flicks with his wrist and suddenly all the dry, crumbly bits are mixed in. "It's like I said." He flashes me his hideous grin. "A light hand."

I put the biscuits on a baking tray and pop them into the oven. "Who taught you how to do that?" I ask.

"My late wife."

His late wife? I turn away from Geezer. I start wiping the counter.

I think about the photo hanging in the living room. About the woman with the brown-grey hair and the blue eyes. She looks like she was starting to laugh when someone snapped the picture. I've looked at it lots of times over the past few weeks. I've thought about asking who it was, but I didn't know if that would be okay. I still don't know for sure but —

"So the picture out there —" I point toward the living room.

Geezer nods. "Yes. My darling Kathleen."

Then neither of us says anything. While I'm washing the mixing bowl, I start thinking about Geezer being married to someone. I guess I shouldn't be so surprised about that since he's a grandfather. And now I'm wondering why Lucas is living with Geezer. He wouldn't be my first choice. Then again with Mom out of the picture, I'm not getting my first choice either.

I check the oven clock while I finish wiping the counter. It's time for me to leave.

"Hang on," Geezer says. "The scones are nearly done. You can take some home. Test them out yourself. That way if you break a tooth, it's your own damn fault."

He points toward a kitchen drawer. "Grab a paper plate." I hand one to him and he transfers some of the hot scones onto it.

"Do you need me to warm up the chicken stew before I take off?" I ask.

"Yep," he says. "Put that casserole dish into the microwave and set it for six minutes. Lucas and me — we'll take it from there."

Aunt Sarah and the twins are surprised when I show up with warm, homemade biscuits. I still can't believe Geezer can make something this good. I think back to when Mom and I lived together. We never made anything homemade at all — like with actual ingredients.

Carter interrupts my thoughts. "This *so* yummy!"

"Maybe I can show you how to make them someday," I say.

"Yes!" Carter and Lawson are both jumping on their chairs.

"But," I say, "you have to mix everything together with a light hand. Otherwise the biscuits get too hard. You don't want to break a tooth when you're eating them, right?"

"No!" Lawson stuffs his hand into his mouth and starts feeling his teeth.

"And leave me a few, okay?" I say. "I want some for later when I'm studying."

⁕⁕⁕

The unit test I have coming up in Biology messes with my head for the rest of the week. It's been a while since I've needed to learn this much stuff. Plus, I never used to study for tests. I just went in cold and took my chances.

It doesn't settle my nerves at all when I spot Fletch and the Clones while I'm at my locker. They keep muttering about me disrespecting them and their future gang brothers. Of course, they say it just loud enough that I can't miss it while I'm on my way to class. I try to ignore them. Right now, I need to focus on Bio. Once I'm farther into the course, Finn wants me to start Grade Eleven Business too.

Finn knows I've been nervous about the test. He helped me make study cards earlier this week. We're going to get some extra practice in before I take the test. That means I'll be leaving school later than usual today. This is also my last day to get Lucas home and to help out at Geezer's house. At first, I wasn't sure how that would work. But then Geezer said he'd pick up Lucas after school himself. I'll go help out at his house after I've finished the exam.

I try to block everything out while I read over the test questions. So far, it's going okay. I try not to freak out when I hit some harder questions. I'll come back to those later. By the time I've answered the easier questions and doubled back to the harder ones, I've calmed down a bit. Even if I screw up on some of them, I'm pretty sure I'll still pass. I might even get a decent mark.

I read over my answers one last time like Finn told me to. By then, I'm ready to leave. It's way too quiet in here without Slater snapping his gum, and without Nina announcing whenever the alien goth child backflips across her bladder.

"I'm done," I tell Finn.

"That's great," he smiles. "We'll have the results soon. You studied hard for that, Zaine. You should be proud of yourself."

I'm not used to people saying nice things about me. My face burns bright red. "Better wait until we get the mark back," I say. "See you tomorrow."

I drop off some stuff at my locker. I'm heading toward the main entrance when I hear voices. One belongs to Fletch. I'm sure his clones are nearby too.

Then I hear Lucas. What's that about?

I turn down the hallway. What I see makes me feel sick to my stomach.

Chapter 16

Obstacle Course

Garbage cans, textbooks, T-shirts, papers —
Fletch, Bryce, and Skeeter are shoving all those
things at Lucas. They've turned the hall into
an obstacle course. Lucas is doing his best to
manoeuvre around everything on his crutches.
Fletch and the Clones are laughing their
stupid heads off the whole time.

But I don't get this. Where's Geezer? He
was supposed to have picked up Lucas an hour
ago. What do I do now? If I step in, these guys

might seriously hurt Lucas.

They slide a heavy textbook across the floor at Lucas. I cringe when it bangs against his foot. Fletch and the Clones laugh and shove the garbage can into him again. It lands against his knee — right by where the empty pant-leg is pinned back. Lucas cries out in pain. In some ways, he is even more vulnerable than I was the night I got attacked under the bridge.

Just then, one of Lucas's crutches lands on a navy-blue T-shirt. My heart nearly stops as he skids sideways. He barely keeps his balance, but the crutch flies from his hand. Skeeter kicks it down the hall. The rubber end of it bounces off of my running shoe in the doorway that I've slipped into.

"Let's see how well you manage the hall now," Skeeter says.

That's it! I've seen enough!

I step out into the middle of the hallway. "Try that again and I'll kick all your asses." My voice is tight and low.

Fletch and the Clones turn. Their eyes are wide when they see me. I'm gripping Lucas's crutch like it's a baseball bat that I'm about to swing at their heads. That's definitely something I could do right now.

Fletch scowls. "You think you can disrespect us? You're gonna learn otherwise!"

He comes toward me. I tighten my grip on the crutch. I can't wait to take the first swing at him!

Then footsteps echo from the stairwell. Fletch backs away from me. Apparently he doesn't feel like sticking around to have a witness see what they're doing.

"Good thing your big brother showed up, Cripple," he calls to Lucas.

"You're not gonna be so lucky next time," Bryce adds. "Just wait."

"Come on, boys." Fletch starts running. "We've got a long night ahead of us."

They disappear down the far staircase. I hand Lucas back his crutch. I've just gathered up the textbooks and T-shirts when Mrs. Tang appears.

"You boys are here later than usual," she says. "Everything okay?"

I glance at Lucas to see if he's going to say anything about Fletch and the Clones. He gives me a quick shake of his head.

"I had an exam to write," I say. "We were just leaving."

She raises an eyebrow. When neither of us says anything else, she eventually turns and walks back the way she came. Her heels clatter as she makes her way down the hall.

Meanwhile, my mind is tripping over what Fletch said about me being Lucas's big brother. I've hardly even thought of myself as Carter and Lawson's big brother, much less Lucas's.

Then I look back over at Lucas. He's wiping his face with the sleeve of his T-shirt. He looks paler than ever, and he's shaking.

"No offence, Lucas," I say, "but you don't

look so great." The door to the next classroom is open. "Come sit down in here."

As soon as he's inside, Lucas drops into the nearest chair.

"Thanks," he says. "For helping me out back there."

I nod. "Do they hassle you like that all the time?"

Lucas runs his hand through his hair. "Not all the time. I'm an easy target with just one leg. But I knew that would be the case when I decided to go ahead with the amputation. Still, it sucks."

"Wait a second," I say. "You mean, you *chose* to have your leg amputated?"

"Yeah," Lucas says. "Most people think I lost it because of cancer or a car accident. But I was born with a deformed foot. The doctors wanted to remove it when I was a baby. They said it would get worse and cause me a lot of pain. But my parents thought it was too soon. They were afraid I'd resent them later on for making that choice for me." He takes another deep breath.

"It turned out the doctors were right," he continues. "My foot was growing funny and that leg was way shorter than the other one. I wore a brace for a while, but it didn't really help. It just hurt, and it slowed me down. So along with the doctors and my parents, I finally decided the bottom part of my leg had to go."

"Um, your *parents*?" I ask. "But you live with your grandfather, so —"

Lucas's face clouds over. "My parents are living in Ecuador. They'd always wanted to work overseas. But when the chance finally came along, the amputation was already set up. We thought there was enough time for me to have the surgery and to heal from it so I could get a prosthetic leg. But then my leg got infected. I couldn't travel to Ecuador with my parents after all. I had to move in with my grandfather instead.

"Mom and Dad finish their jobs in Ecuador in four months. If my leg heals in time and I'm getting around okay, I'll go join them.

Otherwise, I'll stick around here till they get back."

I'm still trying to process all of that when I hear lopsided footsteps, then cursing. That could only be Geezer. I look out the door. He has Lucas's wheelchair with him. Thank god for that.

"In here," I call out. "Lucas just needed to sit down for a bit."

Geezer gives me a sheepish look. "I can't believe I fell asleep."

"I can't believe you admitted it." I smile and take the wheelchair from him.

Geezer gives me a semi-pissed-off look as I bring the chair over to Lucas. We make our way out to Geezer's car together. It's a shiny red hatchback.

"Nice car!" I say.

"You sound surprised," Geezer says. "What did you expect?"

"Actually a beaten-up old junker, kind of like —" I stop myself just in time.

"Kind of like *me*?" Geezer asks.

"Hey, you said it. Not me."

We soon arrive at Geezer's house. That means I have to do the job I've been putting off for five weeks. I have to clean out the shed where this all started. That place meant a lot to me back when Rob was around and I needed to go cool off. I really don't want to see the mess I left it in.

Lucas goes inside the house. Geezer follows me around to the backyard. I grit my teeth and open the shed door.

"It's almost empty!" I say. "Where did everything go?"

"I needed to clean out a bunch of crap anyway," Geezer mutters. "While I was at it, I went ahead and fixed the lock on the door too."

"I thought we were going to call in a locksmith."

"Whatever," Geezer says. "Half the time, those so-called 'professionals' do a slap-happy job. Then they charge you a big price for it. I was better off doing it myself."

He points toward the garage. "Look inside the door," he says. "I left you some paint and a brush."

As I'm opening the can of paint, I realize Geezer saved me a bunch of money by not hiring a locksmith. He also repaired the door frame. It doesn't take me long to paint it.

As I step back inside the house, I glance at the clock. I can hardly believe the five weeks are nearly over. The only thing left is the final meeting tomorrow. After that, I wonder how Geezer is going to get Lucas home from school. Geezer looks a bit stronger, but Lucas sure doesn't.

"Do you guys have stuff for supper?" I ask.

"Yep," Geezer says. "We'll heat up the leftover roast beef."

"No scones today?"

"Nope." Geezer shakes his head. "We're all set."

"Okay." I'm shuffling my feet by the door. "I guess I'm done then. So, I'll see you tomorrow at the meeting."

I glance over at Lucas. Even though that meeting is about him too, I never asked Lucas if he wants to join us. He beats me to it.

"I'm gonna come too," Lucas says. "Like, if that's okay."

"Sure," I say. "I'll see you there."

While I'm walking home, I think back to the first meeting. Lucas hadn't come to it because he didn't give a shit about me, as Geezer said. I'd felt the same way about him. That's kind of funny now, considering I was ready to kick the crap out of Fletch and the Clones for Lucas earlier today. If I hadn't been able to stop them, I don't know what I might have done.

Maybe this is what it feels like every day for people who have a real family.

Chapter 17

Long Night Ahead

"I'm glad your Bio test went well," Aunt Sarah says as we clean up after dinner. "Mrs. Kriegson is going to babysit again tomorrow while we're at the meeting with Constable Haddad."

I turn to Carter and Lawson. "You guys will be on your best behaviour, right?"

Lawson nods.

"Why?" Carter asks.

Aunt Sarah laughs. "You can think about that while you're putting on your PJs."

It's only after the twins and Aunt Sarah have gone to bed that Fletch and the Clones' words push their way back into my head again.

Just wait.

Good thing your big brother showed up, Cripple. You're not gonna be so lucky next time.

Next time.

My heart speeds up. All along, it felt like they were yelling at me. First, because I wouldn't join the gang with them. Then, because I stuck up for Lucas. But really, they were yelling those words at Lucas.

I remember something else they'd said about Geezer and Lucas a few days back. *We could all go break into his house.*

And what else did Fletch say today?

We've got a long night ahead of us, boys.

Oh my god! Is that what they're planning to do tonight? Break into Geezer and Lucas's house? After what I saw today, I wouldn't put it past them. Something suddenly becomes clear to me. My quiet night at home just took a different turn.

Up until now, my curfew was no big deal. I didn't have any friends to go out with anyway. But tonight, the curfew matters. I've got to break it. Even if it means I get kicked out of the house.

I pause to take a few deep breaths. Then I lift the curtain and slide my bedroom window open. The screen has never fit properly. It pops out right away when I shove a pair of scissors under the window frame. I set the screen outside on the grass. As I step through the window, I check the time. It's almost ten o'clock. I'm already violating my probation.

That's okay, I tell myself. *All I'm doing is walking down the street. That's not illegal.*

Then again, it probably *is* illegal since the cops gave me a nine o'clock curfew.

I circle around behind the house. I take the back alley to the end of our block before I step onto the sidewalk. I'm trying not to look suspicious, except I don't know how to do that. I try to copy the people I see across the street. I stand up straighter. I loosen my arms and let them swing at my sides. I slow down. I never would have thought that looking relaxed was so hard.

My head is spinning. What if I didn't need to come out tonight at all? What if I'm risking getting kicked out of the house for nothing? Maybe I should just turn around and go back home.

Then again, Fletch and the Clones might have already gone to Geezer's place. I have to keep going. I don't have enough proof to go call the cops. Maybe they wouldn't believe me anyway after all the trouble I've been in. But I need to check in on Geezer and Lucas. I need to know they're okay.

I slip behind the plaza. As I step into the ravine, my ears are tuned to every little scurry in the bushes. I force myself to slow down so I'm walking as quietly as I can. I'm finally by the same fence where I threw the wrench all those weeks ago. That's when I hear footsteps.

I slip deeper into the woods and crouch down behind some pine trees. In the darkness, I can see three people. And I can almost hear the sneers in their voices.

". . . old guy with a cast . . . kid with one leg . . . easy targets."

And last of all: "Zaine's going down."

A wave of rage washes over me. My heart is racing. Even though they have me outnumbered, I'm ready to take on all three of them right here. To take them by surprise.

But it's too soon. So far, they haven't done anything wrong. Unlike me, they're not even breaking curfew.

With no warning at all, they rush straight for Geezer's back door. Glass shatters against the steps. Suddenly, they're inside. *Shit!* I wish I had a cell phone so I could call the cops.

Then again, that wouldn't work anyway. If I made the call, they'd know it came from me. They'd know I was breaking my curfew!

I sneak around to the side window. In the darkened room, I can see one guy rummaging around. Moments later, he holds up a bottle of booze. That's definitely Fletch. It seems that he and the Clones are trying to be heard. I don't get that, but it might work in my favour. Hopefully Geezer or the neighbours will hear them and call the cops. Then I can just go home. Nobody would even have to know I left my house tonight.

One of the Clones grabs the bottle from Fletch and takes a swig. Then he gives a loud *whoop*.

Fletch grabs the bottle back. He smashes it against the side of the TV. "Here, Zaine!" he yells. "This one's for you, buddy!"

An upstairs light blinks on just as I realize what Fletch and the Clones are doing. They're making it look like I'm involved in the break-in. They're trying to get me arrested again.

The next thing I know, Geezer is thundering down the wooden staircase. He has a crutch in one hand and his cast is bouncing against each step.

"Stay in your room, Lucas!" he yells.

As soon as Geezer says Lucas's name, the scene from the school hall flashes before me again. Lucas stumbling over the obstacles they'd pitched at him. The ugly name they'd pitched at him too. *Cripple.*

Next thing I know, my feet have landed on the back porch. If there was ever a time for me not to get involved, it's long gone.

Chapter 18

Uppercut

Geezer is swinging his crutch at Fletch. Skeeter is right behind them. I grab Skeeter and fling him to the ground. His head smacks against the hardwood floor.

Geezer's eyes widen when he sees me. Fletch follows Geezer's gaze. His face freezes in shock. Then Geezer, with about a million years of boxing experience, takes advantage of Fletch looking the other way. He throws an uppercut to Fletch's chin. Fletch drops to the floor.

Skeeter is getting back onto his feet. I'm grabbing him again when I see Bryce. He's hauled Lucas to the top of the stairs.

"Look who I found!" he yells.

Lucas is clutching the railing, just barely standing up.

I decide on the spot that Geezer will have to fend for himself. Even with a cast on his ankle, it looks like he's got it pretty much covered.

I shove Skeeter out of the way. Then I take two, maybe three, steps at a time. I'm halfway up the stairs when Bryce pulls hard on Lucas's arm. Lucas's hand slides from the railing and he starts to fall. His body slams against each step as he flails around for something to grab onto. I pause halfway up the stairs to stop his fall. I'll come back to help Lucas later. Right now, my eyes are fixed on the back of Bryce. He's running like hell across the upper landing to get away from me. He better run because when I catch him —

An explosion of sirens and lights and shouts breaks out behind me.

"*Freeze!*" someone yells.

I skid to a halt. Behind me, Lucas is still moaning in pain. I turn and start walking down the stairs toward him.

"I said '*FREEZE*!'"

A cop rushes at me, his flashlight held overhead. I imagine it crashing into the side of my head as he grabs my arm. Another cop hops over Lucas and runs upstairs. From the scuffling and the muted cries coming from Bryce, I know he's been caught. Just like Skeeter, whose face is bleeding. The blood on the end of Geezer's crutch pretty much tells me what happened there. Fletch is just starting to move.

The other cop is still holding on to me. I try to pull away and he grabs me tighter and rougher.

"You heard me say 'freeze!'" the cop yells in my face. "Don't move!"

I suddenly realize what's going on. They

think I'm with Fletch and the Clones.

I need Geezer and Lucas to speak up for me. Then again, they haven't always been my biggest fans. What if they don't?

A heavy silence seems to have filled the room while I stand there frozen. My heart is pounding like crazy.

Come on! Just tell the cops, okay?

"That one," Geezer points at me. "He was helping us."

Oh, thank god!

The cop takes his hands off of me. I think I'm allowed to un-freeze. I take slow steps down the stairs — my legs heavier than ever.

I tuck my hand under Lucas's arm. "I've got you," I say. "Let's go downstairs."

I'm holding up Lucas as he hops down one step at a time. Geezer watches us the whole way. When we finally drop down onto the couch, Geezer hobbles over to his battered old chair and sits down too.

Two other cops soon arrive. Some

paramedics show up next. They check out Fletch and Bryce.

One of the cops turns and looks at me. "You're Haddad's kid, right?" she says.

"Um, what?" Then I recognize her. Constable Persaud. The same cop who read me my rights all those weeks ago.

"You're working with Constable Haddad on that restorative-justice project, right?" she asks.

"Oh. Yeah."

Constable Persaud turns to the other officers. "I'll take Zaine's statement," she says. "Then I'll drive him home."

As Fletch and the Clones leave with some police officers, Skeeter — in his nasally voice — is whining about how the break-in is their gang initiation. About how he didn't want to do it but his friends made him. From what I've seen of him, that's pretty hard to believe.

"It sounds like these boys have been busy. Gang brothers." Constable Persaud shakes her head. "The initiations alone are brutal. Getting beaten up to show how tough you are, or committing a robbery, or a home break-in."

A home break-in. Like what they did tonight. They were trying to see to their gang initiation and to get back at me at the same time.

"But that's not your problem, Zaine," Constable Persaud says. "Let's just get you home."

It takes more effort than I thought to stand up.

"You guys still okay for the meeting tomorrow?" I ask Lucas and Geezer.

"Yeah," Lucas says. "I guess I'm tougher than they thought."

"Smarter too," Constable Persaud says. "Your timing on making that phone call was perfect."

So it was Lucas who called the cops? A smile appears across Geezer's battered old face.

"See you in the morning," he says. "Nine o'clock. Sharp. I can drive you and your aunt if you like."

My whole body feels exhausted. "That'd be great," I say. My hand shakes as I write my address onto a pad of paper by Geezer's phone.

I step outside then I slide into the police car with Constable Persaud. She asks me a bunch of questions about Fletch, Skeeter, and Bryce. When she's taken my statement, she drives me to Aunt Sarah's place.

"This house here?" Constable Persaud asks.

"Yeah," I say. "I live with my aunt and my little cousins."

For now, I think. When Aunt Sarah finds out I broke curfew —

"I need to release you back into your aunt's care," Constable Persaud says. "They reminded me when I called the station that you have a curfew."

I trudge to the front door with Constable Persaud. "I, um, don't have my key with me." That seems a better thing to say than *I ripped out the window screen so I could sneak out after my curfew.*

She reaches around me and rings the

doorbell. In the darkness, it sounds like a cannon going off.

A moment later, a light blinks on. Aunt Sarah appears at the window beside the front door. The expression on her face shifts to alarm when she sees me outside with a cop.

"Oh no, Zaine!" she cries. "Not again!"

"Can I step inside for a moment, ma'am?" Constable Persaud says.

Aunt Sarah stands aside, clutching her nightgown against her.

"Were you aware that Zaine was out after curfew tonight?" Constable Persaud asks.

"No." Aunt Sarah shakes her head. "No, I wasn't."

I'm glad Constable Persaud explains what happened. There's no way I could piece everything together and say it in a way that makes any sense.

"Your nephew intervened to keep Mr. Giezenman and his grandson from getting harmed," Constable Persaud says. "Still,

Constable Haddad will want to talk about it further with Zaine." She turns back toward me. "There are to be no more curfew breaches until the entire restorative agreement has been fulfilled. That includes after Constable Haddad has spoken with the judge about whether they'll drop the charges. Do you understand?"

I nod. "Yes."

Aunt Sarah closes the door. Then she looks at me for a long moment. "Are you hurt?" she asks.

I shake my head.

"Are Mr. Giezenman and Lucas okay?"

"A bit banged up," I say. "But they're mostly okay too."

The room does a little wobble.

"So is the meeting still on for tomorrow?" Aunt Sarah asks.

"Yeah," I nod. "If it's okay, can we talk later? Because right now —"

"Zaine," Aunt Sarah says, "sometimes I don't know what to do with you."

Oh no. Here it comes!

"Like tonight," she says. "Part of me wants to throttle you for sneaking out. But the bigger part of me is so proud of you that I can hardly stand it."

She pulls me into a tight hug. Aunt Sarah is a lot shorter than me. I'm glad that she's not telling me to grab my stuff and leave. But my back is ready to snap in two from being all hunched over like this. When Aunt Sarah lets go of me, she's wiping her eyes.

"Go to bed," she says. "We both need to get some sleep before the meeting tomorrow morning."

Chapter 19

Brand-New Start

I nearly jump through the ceiling when my alarm goes off. It was late when I finally fell asleep last night. Whenever I wasn't thinking about Lucas or about Fletch and the Clones, I was worrying about the meeting this morning.

Because it's Saturday morning, the twins get to watch TV in the living room while they eat their cereal. I stumble past them into the kitchen. I try to swallow some toast, but my stomach is in knots. I'm also wondering if Geezer and Lucas are doing okay.

"You haven't eaten much." Aunt Sarah frowns.

"I'm not too hungry," I say.

My legs are shaky as I take my plate over to the dishwasher. Maybe some fresh air would help.

"I'll go wait outside," I say.

Aunt Sarah is standing by the sink finishing her coffee. "Mrs. Kriegson is on her way over. I'll join you in a few minutes."

I call a 'goodbye' to the twins. I'm almost down the steps when a car pulls up. I'm walking toward it but then I stop. This isn't Geezer's car.

A moment later, a woman steps out of the rusty, yellow sedan. "Zaine, honey!"

My entire body seizes up. All I can do is stare at the woman with the long, sandy-coloured hair and that wide, toothy grin. It's the face I tried to remember all those nights when I was afraid I'd forgotten what she even looked like.

"Are you surprised, Zaine?" Mom wraps me in a tight hug. "I got into town late last night. I stayed with some friends because I wanted to surprise you this morning. You know, to make up for the last time we talked."

She takes a step back and looks at me like she's waiting for me to burst into song or something. "Hey," she says. "Isn't it great to see your mom?"

"Yeah." I say. "So, where is he?"

"Who?" Mom asks.

"Your special new guy."

Mom's gaze drops to the sidewalk. "That didn't quite work out. But that's for the best. That's what brought me back here with you." Then she flashes me a big smile. "And you know, I decided something. That we're not going to stay in Melton Grove. We're going to make a brand-new start in a brand-new city. Doesn't that sound exciting?"

She hardly even pauses to catch her breath. "My friend Julianne — the one I borrowed the car from — lives near Vancouver. I have to get the car back to her tonight. So we need to load up your things and get on our way. And from Vancouver, we could keep going on to Victoria. What do you think of that?"

Victoria? Jeez, I don't know. That's pretty far from Aunt Sarah and the twins. Then again, maybe a new start is exactly what I need.

Just then, another car pulls up. Geezer rolls the window down. "Come on," he yells. "We've got a meeting to go to."

"Mom," I say, "I need to go."

"But I promised I'd get the car back to Julianne tonight. We've got a twelve-hour drive ahead of us."

I give Geezer a wave to show him I'm coming.

"We'll have to talk about that later, Mom," I say.

"Zaine, why are you brushing me off? I've come all this way to see you — so we can start a new life together."

My thoughts are swirling all over the place. Part of me wants to yell, *It's been four years, Mom! What took you so long?* The other part of me wants to ditch the meeting and take off with Mom before she changes her mind.

"Get a move on!" Geezer shouts.

My head is swiveling from Mom to Geezer, then back to Mom.

"I've got a meeting to go to," I finally say. "I can't just leave with you. At least not until afterwards. Even then —"

I don't know what comes next in that sentence. But I don't think Mom heard me anyway.

"Hurry the hell up!" Geezer shouts.

"Go grab your things," Mom says at the same time. "So we can get going."

"But, Mom, this meeting is important," I say.

"One minute!" Geezer's head is sticking

out the window. "If we're not outta here in one minute, we're gonna be late!"

Mrs. Kriegson is watching us as she climbs up the steps of the house. And now Geezer is honking the horn!

"Mom, it's not just any meeting. It's —"

How do I explain this in less than one minute?

I can't.

"Go inside, Mom. Aunt Sarah and the twins are there. I'll be home in a couple of hours."

Aunt Sarah appears at the door. Her reaction to Mom is the same as mine was. Mouth open. Eyes wide.

"Aunt Sarah, can you stay here with Mom? Please?"

"Zaine, I need to be at this meeting too because —"

"But I need you to stay with Mom," I say.

"I'm coming to the meeting," Aunt Sarah says, "and that's final."

Geezer is laying on the horn now.

I wave my arm toward him. "I'm coming!"

Mom still looks baffled about why I haven't left with her already. But I can't just leave her here without Aunt Sarah or me being here too. What if she takes off before we get back? And I can't let her come with us. If she hears about the charges that got laid against me, she'll *never* want to live with me.

Then another thought pushes its way into my head. Mom has missed out on a lot of my life. Maybe it's time to be honest with her. To let her catch up on some of the parenting stuff she's missed.

"Actually, Mom," I say, "You need to come too."

Then I don't give her time to answer. I lean into Geezer's car window. "Thanks for coming here to get me," I tell him. "We'll meet you at school instead."

"Whatever, kid," Geezer says. "Just hurry the hell up."

Chapter 20

Beth

"Come on, Mom," I say. "I need you to come with Aunt Sarah and me."

"Okay, I'll come with you." Mom shrugs. "We'll take Julianne's car. That way we can leave right away after your 'important meeting.'"

I don't comment on that last part. While we drive to the school, I want to explain to Mom what's happened. But she doesn't give me the chance. She keeps chattering about how her friend, Julianne, will freak out if Mom doesn't get the car back soon. Then she describes the drive from Vancouver. By the time she's finished talking about the mountain views and about the elk and the black bear she saw on her way through Jasper National Park, we're at school.

As we walk in, I try to prepare Mom. "So, this meeting," I say. "It's because I got in some trouble a while back."

"Really?" Mom asks. "How much trouble could you have gotten in?"

I glance sideways at Aunt Sarah. "Actually, quite a lot. That's why we're having this meeting — to see about getting some charges against me dropped."

"Oh, for god's sake," Mom says. "You're a kid. Kids get in trouble all the time."

Lucas and Geezer are making their way across the school parking lot. They're moving slower than usual. It doesn't take long to catch up with them.

"Hey," I say. "This is my mom and my aunt Sarah."

"Yes, I'm Beth." Mom smiles. "It's so nice to meet Zaine's friends. And you two are —"

"Mr. Giezenman," I say. "And that's Lucas. Lucas and I are in the same program at school."

"Wonderful!" Mom says. "Lucas, you'll have to fill me in on what my son has been up to since I last saw him."

You'd better brace yourself, Mom!

As we walk in, Mom is rattling on about Vancouver and about the new life she's been trying to "launch" — whatever that means.

"You okay, Lucas?" I ask.

"Mostly," Lucas says.

"This is such fun getting the tour of my son's school," Mom says.

I point toward the staffroom door. "We're meeting in here," I say.

"Ooh, fancy." Mom reads the sign. "I always wondered where the teachers hang out. When they aren't terrorizing the students, that is."

We step into the staffroom together. Constable Haddad — who's left his cop uniform at home for a change — and Football Guy are already there. So is Finn.

"It looks like we have a guest today," Constable Haddad says. "Can you do the introductions, Zaine?"

"This is my mom, Beth Wyatt," I say. "She just got into town."

"Were you away on a business trip or something?" Lucas asks.

My ears are tuned to how Mom is going to answer.

"Sort of," she says. "Zaine and I are actually leaving for Vancouver today. Right after this meeting is over."

Finn and Constable Haddad both shoot me a look. I don't know what to say, so I just keep my jaw clamped shut.

For someone who says she wants this meeting to finish quickly, Mom is sure taking a lot of time. She's babbling away about her travels through British Columbia, and about all the fascinating people she's met there.

I lean over in my chair. "We need to start the meeting, Mom."

"Oh gosh. Of course." She sounds surprised that this isn't just a nice social get-together.

Constable Haddad begins. "Most of us here — except for Lucas and Ms. Wyatt —"

"Oh, you can call me 'Beth.'"

"— except for Lucas and *Beth* attended our previous meeting on April fourteenth. At that time, we discussed Zaine's actions. They resulted in him being charged with break and enter, mischief, theft, and assault causing bodily harm."

I glance at Mom. I'm trying to gauge her reaction to hearing these charges. But she's still wearing the same fixed smile.

"I took on the role of Zaine's probation officer," Constable Haddad continues. "While Zaine was not particularly forthcoming with me, he met briefly with me every day as required.

"Zaine was also given a nine o'clock curfew. He respected that curfew until last night. I'm not fully in favour of Zaine's decision to leave his home without first discussing it with his aunt. However, Zaine assisted Mr. Giezenman and Lucas during a break-in at their home. I understand they could both have sustained more serious injury if Zaine had not stepped in on their behalf."

"Oh, Zaine!" Mom says. "I'm so proud of you for sticking up for your friends like that." My face burns bright red as she clasps me to her in a big hug.

Constable Haddad pauses. "Since our first meeting, Zaine has helped Lucas get home from school each day. He has also done various housekeeping and cooking duties. He further repaired the damage he caused in Mr. Giezenman's garden shed.

"On the face of it," he says, "it appears that Zaine has lived up to all of his responsibilities."

Something about the way he says that makes my stomach lurch. It doesn't feel quite right.

"Part of my duty next week is to recommend to the Court whether they should consider dismissing the charges against Zaine. But there's a problem: I still can't decide whether they should do that or not."

What? After everything I've done?

I feel as though I just got the wind knocked out of me. It's like I'm back under the bridge with the guy pounding on me again.

I look over at Mom. After four long years away, I need her to speak up. Like, right now.

Come on, Mom. Just do this one thing for me, okay?

Chapter 21

After All

Come on, Mom. Right now!

I need Mom to explain that she hasn't been around for four years. That it's one of the main reasons I've landed in so much trouble. But instead, she's checking the time and looking around the room. I'm so focused on Mom that I hardly notice Aunt Sarah is speaking beside me.

"Zaine has done everything required of him," she says. "He has done it completely on his own. And these last few months have been hard for us.

"My husband — soon to be my *ex*-husband — kicked Zaine out of our house. When Zaine returned to my house, he had been badly beaten. But he started back to school and he's been doing well there. He probably doesn't realize that he's setting a good example for my three-year-old twins."

I blink back some tears while Aunt Sarah's words sink in.

Finn speaks next. "I agree with Sarah," he says. "Zaine has been working hard at school. He's making excellent progress and getting good marks."

Mom leans toward Finn. "Well, I'm sure it's because he has a good teacher," she smiles. "Wouldn't you agree?"

I cringe as I realize something. Mom is flirting with Finn. She's actually *flirting* with my teacher!

"Not at all." Finn's voice is cool. "Zaine

has been doing his course fully online. He's been basically teaching himself. Aside from suggesting some study techniques, I've had very little to do with Zaine's success."

"Oh." Mom's smile freezes.

"What are your thoughts, Lucas?" Constable Haddad asks. "I understand that Zaine has been helping you and your grandfather while you've been working through some health issues."

"Yeah, I had part of my right leg amputated a few months ago." Lucas's voice cracks as he says that. "It hasn't healed as well as the doctors thought it would."

"Wouldn't you know it!" Mom shakes her head. "Things are never as simple as you'd think. But I've learned something over the years — that you just have to keep moving forward." She smiles at Lucas. "I understand exactly what you're going through."

I cringe again in my chair.

"You understand *exactly* what I'm going

through?" Lucas says. "So, when are you getting *your* leg amputated?"

Geezer gives a loud snort.

"Lucas," Constable Haddad tries to get us back on track. "Was Zaine helpful to you these past five weeks?"

I think back to how Lucas wouldn't accept my help in the beginning. We've come a long way since he whipped his glasses case at me. I hold my breath, waiting to see if Lucas mentions the other stuff. The good stuff.

"Yeah," he says. "Zaine helped me a lot. Like when Fletch and his two buddies were picking on me in the hall."

"What? Those three punks have harassed you before?" Geezer sputters.

Lucas flushes. So do I. It's not so long ago that Geezer was talking about me that way too.

"I'll make a note of that, Lucas. We can chat further about the previous harassment problems," Constable Haddad says. "That brings me to you, Mr. Giezenman. Do you feel like

Zaine has made up for the harm he caused you?"

Geezer hesitates for a moment. "I didn't think much of this kid in the beginning," he says. "But I've changed my mind about him."

A warmth spreads through me. Beside me, Aunt Sarah is wiping her eyes.

"Okay then." Mom checks the time again. "I guess the meeting is over, right?"

"Not quite." Constable Haddad flips through his notes. "I'd like to remind the group about an exchange from the previous meeting several weeks ago. At that time, Zaine apologized to you, Mr. Giezenman. But you were not willing to accept his apology. Do you feel any differently now?"

Geezer starts nodding his head. I need to speak up fast.

"Actually," I say, "I don't want you to accept that apology."

Around the room, everyone is staring at me. I can tell they're confused by what I just said.

"I remember that day well," I say. "When I

said I was sorry back then, I didn't really mean it. I was just trying to get out of trouble.

"But this is the real apology." I turn and look Geezer right in the eye. "I'm really sorry. I'm sorry that I broke into your shed and trashed your stuff — even though you said later that it was mostly 'a bunch of old crap anyway.'

"And you were right that I should have owned up to what I did at the time. That way, you wouldn't have gotten hurt when I ran away and threw the wrench." I pause to catch my breath. "I know that I'm officially done helping you and Lucas after school. But I'll keep doing it. If you want me to, that is."

Aunt Sarah is sobbing now.

"Thanks, kid," Geezer says. "You're okay after all. Who the hell would've guessed that? Lucas and me, we'll talk later about whether to take you up on that extra help or not."

A slow smile is growing across Constable Haddad's face. "Since everyone has decided that you're 'okay after all,' Zaine, I've decided too.

I'll recommend that the Court drop the charges against you. Especially since you've fulfilled the terms of the contract and you've shown remorse for what you did. Also on the endorsement of the victim, Mr. Giezenman.

"It's of course still up to the Court to make the final decision. But I'm quite confident they will dismiss the charges."

Suddenly I feel weak all over. I look around me. There aren't many dry eyes in the room.

"At this time," Constable Haddad says, "I'll draw this meeting to a close."

"Oh, good!" Once again, Mom's voice is too loud and too cheery. "We need to get on our way, Zaine. Look at the time!"

Mom stands up and rushes from the room. She's partway down the hall before she realizes I've slowed down so Geezer and Lucas can keep up with us.

"We'll be in touch, right?" I say to them when we get to the parking lot.

"Sure thing," Lucas says.

"That is, if you're gonna be sticking around, kid," Geezer adds.

"I'll let you know either way," I say. "And thanks. For everything."

My legs shake as I climb into Julianne's car with Mom and Aunt Sarah.

Chapter 22

Family

Mom hurries up the front steps. "Let's get this show on the road!"

She bursts through the door with Aunt Sarah and me behind her. Carter and Lawson appear a moment later at the kitchen door with Mrs. Kriegson.

"Me having snack." Carter is holding a cup of chocolate milk.

"Careful not to spill it," Aunt Sarah says. "Can you boys say hello to your auntie Beth?"

"Hi," they say. Then they stare at Mom and don't say anything else.

Mom clears her throat. "Um, which one of you is Lawson?" she finally says. "And which one is Carson?"

"This is Lawson," I point. "And that's *Carter*."

"Of course," Mom says. "That's what I meant."

Mrs. Kriegson rolls her eyes. Then she grabs her coat from the back of the couch. "It looks like I'm not needed here anymore."

"Thanks, Eileen," Aunt Sarah says as Mrs. Kriegson takes off out the door.

Mom turns to me. "Just grab what you need from your room, Zaine," she says. "We can get the rest of your stuff shipped out later. Wow, Julianne is going to be super pissed off about me being late with the car."

That's the fifth or sixth time Mom has mentioned Julianne's car. I still don't know how to answer her. Plus it's hitting me that I'm finally getting what I've wanted for four years. I'm getting some time with my mom, even though I didn't expect it to happen quite like this.

That meeting in the staffroom wasn't the best place for a mother-son chat. Still, I keep waiting for Mom to explain some things. Like, why did it take her four years to come see me? And did she miss me?

But she isn't saying anything at all.

Mom is perched on the edge of the couch — crossing then uncrossing her legs. Meanwhile, I'm trying to remember everything I wanted to tell her while she was away. But I don't know how to tell her about those four years. About the school suspensions, and the days and months and years I spent missing her. About the rage and the fights. About living on the streets. About feeling like she had given up on me and I was completely worthless.

I sit down on the couch and face her. "Do you remember what you said on the phone last time, Mom?" I ask. "About how it's best if I keep living with Aunt Sarah and the twins?"

Mom swallows hard and nods.

"I think you were probably right," I say.

Mom's gaze drops down toward her lap. I wait to see if she's going to speak up. But she doesn't.

I look over at Aunt Sarah. "Would it be okay if I stayed? I know the Court hasn't dismissed the charges against me yet. But Constable Haddad said he's pretty sure —"

A loud sob bursts from Aunt Sarah. What does that mean? Does she want me to stay here with her or not?

"Of course it's okay for you to stay here, you ridiculous boy," she says with a sniffle. "Our little family needs you."

'Our little family?' So she actually wants me?

Then Aunt Sarah catches herself. "But it has to be your choice, Zaine."

The silence is heavy in the room. I look sideways at Mom. She has her eyes squeezed shut.

I pause and take a few deep breaths. "That *is* my choice, Aunt Sarah," I say. "To stay here with you and the twins."

Mom opens her eyes. She doesn't look up right away.

"Well. I guess that's my cue to take off." Mom tucks her hair behind her ear and finally looks up.

"You know, Beth," Aunt Sarah's voice is soft, "I've missed you. And before you go, we have some things to discuss."

Aunt Sarah takes out paper and a pen. She asks Mom for some contact names and phone numbers and email addresses. She says she's writing everything down in case Mom's friends or her location "change over time." While they're talking, I think I see for the first time that they really are sisters. Sisters who couldn't be more different. But sisters who love and understand each other. And in their own way, each of them has done the best they could for me.

Mom checks her watch one more time. "Well, I'd better get going."

I follow Mom to the front door. Carter and Lawson are pressed against me on both sides like mini bodyguards. I blink hard to cover the tears I feel forming in my eyes.

"You know, Mom," I say as we step outside, "four years was a long time to go between visits. I'd like you to keep in touch. And I'd like you to come visit me more often."

Mom nods. But even as she's hugging me, I can feel her pulling away. Pulling away from me and back toward her other life in Vancouver or Victoria or wherever she might go next.

"Sure, Zaine." She pats my cheek. "I'll do that. We'll have a good time then, right sweetie?"

"Yeah," I say. "A good time."

Those words remind me of something Mom used to say when I was a lot younger. *I'm always good for a party.*

And it's true. I saw it again today. Mom loves being the life of the party. The centre of

attention. It's all of those other moments —
like most ordinary days — that she's not so
good at.

Before she pulls the car out onto the road,
Mom honks the horn. Her arm is flapping
outside the window in a goodbye wave. Tears
stream down my face.

Mom floors it and the tailpipe cracks
against the curb. It comes partly undone. It's
dragging behind the car — bouncing up and
down against the potholes on the road. Then
the engine gives a load *roar* as Mom does what
she does best. She rides out of town to the next
party.

I turn back toward the house. The twins
are still alongside me. Aunt Sarah is standing
poker-straight by the front steps. I give her a
smile. Then we all step back inside.

Acknowledgements

If not for the generosity and expertise of many people, *Push Back* would never have come to life. Luckily, the right people converged around me at the right times. Many thanks to my dear friend Melody Kohlman, who began this process by listening to my early story ideas, then put me in touch with Lori and Allen Balser.

Following the tragic passing of their son, Andrew Allen Balser (October 18, 1990–July 23, 2005), Lori and Allen opted for restorative justice. Their commitment to responding to their unthinkable loss with compassion instead of with anger continues to inspire me. I will always be grateful, Lori and Allen, for our long conversation in your home while surrounded by photos and mementoes from Andrew's life.

Thanks also to Allen for introducing me to Sue Hopgood and Caroline Missal, a dedicated restorative-justice team. The words of Constable Haddad, my fictitious restorative-justice facilitator, often flowed directly through Sue. I hope that Constable Haddad has made you proud, Sue, and that in some small way, I have as well.

My thanks also to RCMP Superintendent Stacey Talbot, who outlined police procedural matters when placing youths under arrest. Your expertise was invaluable, Stacey, and I am so glad we stopped to admire each other's German Shepherds in the park that day. I continue to cherish the memory of your beloved Ned.

Dr. John Henderson, friend and neighbour, showed extraordinary patience when explaining the medical circumstances relating to the injuries that Zaine and Geezer sustained. Special thanks, John, for pointing me toward the underlying condition that led to Lucas's amputation.

The DTO program that Zaine and Lucas attend is largely a product of my imagination. It was also informed by Susan Yardley's insights into her family's experiences with alternative education. Thank you, Sue. I owe you one.

Matt Spafford continues to advise me about teen culture and phrases. The extended text messages we exchanged while I was writing *Push Back* were invaluable to me. As with everyone else who advised me throughout the writing process, any errors that remain are mine alone.

Many thanks also to the Lorimer team for believing in Zaine and in me, and for including *Push Back* in the wonderful SideStreets series. A special nod to Kat Mototsune — friend, editor, and sensitivity reader — for helping me "revision" this book into another heartfelt project. Kat, it's a pleasure sharing the journey with you.

As always, I am grateful to my darling little family. Many thanks to Ken, Anna, and Shannon. Your love, support, and confidence in me make all the difference.